Publisher's Note

The first series of Frost Hollow books is aimed at boys between the ages of 11 and 15, though as it turns out, girls seem to enjoy them equally. The series is designed to get boys reading, simply by providing stories they can identify with. To that end the stories include sports, adventure, mystery, suspense, and even romance. The themes are drawn from the things boys experience, though events may, from time to time, explode into either myth or fantasy. Each book is a different story with different character,s and no sequels are planned.

These are not "kids" books where everything is age appropriate, because there is no such thing as an age appropriate kid. As a result, the books are not written down, but use complex sentence structure and vocabulary which fit the story and provide some challenge. Nor is there a shortage of the sort of ideas which raise the questions people need to ask. In short, all the elements that any writer of novels uses are used here.

The result is exciting books in which boys are competent, fairminded, ethical, honest, and even heroic. They also screw up.

Finally, it is important to note that the trend in novels for young adult readers has been to produce books which are designed to be discarded. They are printed on the poorest quality paper which yellows and disintegrates over time.

Frost Hollow books cost a little more, but they are printed on high quality, acid-free paper, meaning they will survive rough handling, backpacks, and time.

After all the book you read and like today is not only a book you may well want to read another day, but a book you might wish to save and pass on to your own children. Such things become the threads which bind one generation to another.

Second Printing

Book illustration and design by
Robert J. Benson
Woodland Creative Group
Vermont

Set in Palatino

Copyright 1998 by Robert Holland
Printed in Canada

ISBN 0-9658523-2-6

Summer on Kidd's Creek

A novel of Mystery and Adventure by
Robert Holland

FROST HOLLOW
PUBLISHERS, LLC
Woodstock, Connecticut

More
Books for Boys
By

Robert Holland

The Voice of the Tree
The Purple Car
Footballs Never Bounce True
Breakin' Stones
Eben Stroud
Harry the Hook
Mad Max Murphy
The One-Legged Man Who Came Out of a Well
The Last Champion
Charlie Dollarhide
The Black Queen
Crossing the River
Stealing

Check your local bookseller or order directly from Frost Hollow. Call toll free at 877-974-2081.

All the above titles are $10.95 except for Harry The Hook, which is $11.95. Shipping and handling and sales tax extra.

Also check out our web site at frosthollowpub.com. Read about the books in the series and find out what's coming next.

Chapter 1

Upcreek

Anyone less experienced would most likely have run aground, but Asa Clark knew the channels and side channels in Kidd's Creek as well as any fish. And as he sat in the stern, gripping the handle of the fifteen-horse motor, his eyes traced the darker edges of the main channel. Now and again he adjusted the flight of the trim, fourteen-foot lapstrake skiff, but here, in the middle part of the creek, with the tide still having a long run out, he ran with the engine wide open. The water was deep, twenty feet or better in the channel and the creek ran wide as any river. He suppressed a grin as they came around the turn below the ledges and he changed the angle of the bow ever so slightly.

Ike, fair-haired with pale green eyes, a lean and wiry boy the same age as Asa, at fourteen, sat in the very front of the boat, his back cushioned by his life vest where he rested against the tapering inside point of the bow. Both boys wore vests. The Coast Guard required them, but more to the point, their fathers required them, and getting caught without a vest meant losing the boat. And though they would rather have gone without them on a hot summer day, neither boy considered taking off his vest. On the water you wore a life vest. Only fools thought otherwise, or so they had been taught since they first stepped into a boat.

As they passed The Ledges, Asa eased the boat toward the old white oak that grew on the edge of the right bank. Two summers ago they had tied a rope to the limb that hung out over the creek and once the tide reached its halfway point the water was deep enough so they could swing out over the creek and let go. Usually the rope was tied to the trunk of the tree, but it must have come loose in the wind because now it dangled out over the water. Asa aimed the bow so the fat knot on the rope would conk Ike in the back of the head. Even at this speed it wouldn't hurt, but it would surprise him some, Asa thought, as he watched the rope come closer and closer and then just as it was about to collide with his noggin, Ike ducked and suddenly the rope hung right in front of Asa, and because he had expected quite a different result, he couldn't react fast enough to dodge, and it tunked him squarely in the forehead and knocked his sunglasses onto the floor of the boat.

And then all he could do was laugh along with Ike who clearly thought he had never, no not ever in his life, seen anything so comical. And finally when he began to calm down enough to catch his breath, Asa called out over the drone of the motor. "How did you know when to duck, you creep?"

"I knew you were up to something because you kept edging the boat toward the shore. And then I remembered the rope and I waited till I could see the reflection in those dumb mirror sunglasses."

Asa grinned. One of the best things about having Ike as a friend was the way he could surprise you. Just when you had him figured, he'd do something that caught you unprepared. Best of all he was a good sport. If he'd gotten hit by the rope he'd have laughed just as hard. As they swung past the ledges, Asa scanned the water ahead with greater care. From here on they moved into the shallower water below the curve at East Hook. The channel narrowed and grew less and less predictable in the way it wandered, switching back and forth across the creek.

They watched a snowy egret a hundred yards away, bright white in the sun, picking its way along on black stick legs as it hunted little fish. Sometimes the bird walked quickly to stir up the minnows, stabbing its long bill like a sword, and it always seemed to come up with a fish. Then it would stop to stand on one skinny leg and wait and wait and suddenly stab its bill downward, grab a minnow, and gobble it up.

Both boys liked to watch the creek birds, the ospreys, the egrets, the green herons, and the enormous great blue herons, the shitepokes, that looked as big as the storks in fairy tales. The creek was alive with birds; bitterns, gulls, terns, hawks, eagles, snipe, rail, sandpipers, yellowlegs, black ducks and mallards, and more others than you could count. Underwater it was even busier with hermit crabs running willy nilly in all directions and thousands and thousands of tiny fish following the tides and the big blue crabs scuttling about on the bottom.

Now he ran at half-throttle, following the narrow, twisting channel which showed only as a dark streak where the deeper water absorbed the sunlight and prevented it from reflecting off the bottom the way it did in the shallows. They rode easily along, the boat pushing aside the clear water as the motor forced it upstream against the tide and the current, shoving the bow of the boat up and over the water coming at them.

Ike dangled his hand in the spray as he looked down at the water, watching the reflections of the clouds and thinking, as he did so often, about pirates and particularly about Captain William Kidd and the lost treasure. He'd never doubted that Kidd had buried it here, though everyone told him it was nothing but a legend. And in truth, all his digging around at the library had never turned up a shred of evidence to suggest that Kidd had done anything more than sail up the creek to escape a British man-o'-war. Still, he knew the treasure was here somewhere, buried in the vast marshes, waiting for someone to find it. What an adventure! The search for Kidd's treasure ...

But Ike, who like Asa, had been raised to trust a more practical turn of mind, had another reason as well. He wanted a trail bike, not just any trail bike, but the red Honda down at Bousquet's Motorcycle Shop. Asa wanted the same bike, except in green. Every time they went down to King's Point they went to Bousquet's to look at the bikes. But no kid who came from a fishing family got a present like that. To get those bikes, they'd have to earn the money and that's why they were headed upcreek. The more clams they dug and sold, the more money they made. But it sure would happen faster if they found Kidd's lost treasure.

Asa throttled down the motor as the channel continued

to narrow, holding just enough speed to carry them upstream, and then suddenly the engine sputtered and coughed and he quickly gave it more gas and a cloud of blue oil smoke drifted out over the water.

"You forgot to change the plugs, didn't you," Ike said.

Asa shifted to neutral and revved up the engine trying to burn off the oil which had fouled the spark plugs. "I also put too much oil in when I mixed the gas."

Ike laughed. "Jeez, Asa, that's the kind of stuff I do."

The engine began to run more smoothly and Asa throttled it back and shifted into forward, and despite the risk of running the propeller into the mud, held his speed a little higher.

"Pretty dumb not changing the plugs," he said. "I put two new plugs right out on the work bench where I couldn't miss 'em yesterday afternoon and then forgot all about it."

"We don't have far to go," Ike shouted over the noise from the engine. "And if it won't run later, we'll just row down on the tide."

"I hate rowing," Asa said.

Ike changed the subject before Asa got himself into a full blown grouch. "Do you think Captain Kidd buried his treasure here?" he asked over the drone of the outboard.

"What got you into that again?"

"It's called Kidd's Creek isn't it?"

"Only because he sailed his ship up into the creek once when he was being chased by a British man-o'-war."

"But don't you see? Kidd sailed a sloop and he could have outrun any man-o'-war unless he was carrying a lot of gold to weigh him down. So he sailed into the creek, buried the gold, and then sailed back down, and without all that extra weight all he had to do was get to open water because then the British couldn't catch him."

Asa didn't answer, though he liked the explanation well enough. It made sense. What's more it was just the kind of thing Captain Kidd would have done. Tricky and clever.

"Couldn't have sailed the ship above Boulder Bend," Asa said, "too shallow."

"Sure," Ike said, "but he could've hauled the treasure by long boat from there, and then he could've gone a long way up, probably to The High Ground so the treasure wouldn't get flooded out."

Ike could make the wildest story sound possible and more than once they had gone off on one of his wild chases. But not this time. They had come to dig quahogs in the old clamming ground they hadn't used since last year, and when you went clamming you didn't waste any time or the tide rushed in and put you out of business. Just now the tide had a way to run before it hit dead low. They could begin digging before slack water and still have enough outgoing tide to drift back down. You saved gas that way, and any money they paid for gas cut their profits.

Asa slowed the motor till their speed matched the tide and current, and the boat held steady, neither gaining nor losing as he stood up and checked the channel ahead. Finding treasure sure would beat the heck out of digging clams. So far he had saved only a hundred bucks and that left him a long way from that green Honda. Eleven hundred dollars away. If he was lucky he might make it by the end of next summer, and then he'd be fifteen and he'd only have a year to ride it before he turned sixteen and got his driver's license. Not that he wouldn't still ride it after he got his license, but it wouldn't be the same. He twisted the throttle grip on the motor and the boat moved forward again.

Ike looked over the bow and signaled with his left hand for Asa to steer to port, and Asa brought the boat to the left over a small sandbar and across the channel to the far bank of the creek. Then using the current and the push from the outboard he brought the boat in against the bank and Ike jumped ashore with the anchor.

Neither boy talked now. They muckled onto their clam baskets and rakes and stepped into the knee-deep water, both eager to begin digging. But what once had been as good a bed of clams as you could find on the creek, had not improved by being left alone. They found only cherrystones and a few medium sized quahogs but none of the great old monster quahogs which brought double the going price at those restaurants which specialized in stuffed clams.

Oh, there were clams enough all right but they had come upcreek planning on harvesting a mighty profit. They dug both upstream and downstream along the bank and even waded out chest deep, but the largest clams they found did not measure up.

"Ike?" Asa called as he carried his basket back to the boat, "you find any?"

"No. Just the same old stuff."

"Maybe we ought to go farther upcreek," Asa said.

Ike shook his head as he looked down. "You know the rule. No farther than Boulder Bend."

"Yeah, I know." Asa looked off across the creek at the solid wall of reeds.

"Maybe we could go up to the flats at Boulder Bend," Ike said.

"It's all rocks there and we've tried the flats plenty of times."

"Asa, my father'd probably kill me if he found out I went upcreek."

"Mine too."

"And anyway I'm afraid of going up there."

"But we've been there before," Asa said.

"Yeah, but our fathers took us and they know where the quicksand is and where the holes in the bottom are. Suppose we got stuck in the mud and climbed out to push the boat and got into quicksand. We could be in awful trouble, Asa."

"Okay, okay, I know it's dangerous. But if we stay out of the Fingernails and keep a rope tied around our waists and back to the boat, what can happen?"

"It's just too dangerous." Ike set his clam rake into the boat and hoisted his clam basket, half full of cherrystones, into the boat behind the rake. "All my life people have told stories about men who went up there and never came back, and how they found their boats drifting down the creek on the tide, and how nobody could find the bodies."

"Last fall when we went up duck hunting into the first Fingernail on the right, do you remember the narrow creek going in? Do you remember what the bottom looked like? I know there's quahogs there, Ike, big ones and we can get them."

Ike leaned down onto the boat. "Where would we say we got the clams?"

Asa set his rake in the boat and then lifted his clam basket over the gunwale and set it on the flat duckboard floor. "We can make something up."

"It's risky, Asa."

"Sure it's risky, but we want big clams and that's the only place we haven't tried. If we go now we can make it before the tide turns."

Ike thought about the dirt bike and how much money they could make if they found big quahogs. All the tourists who came through King's Point wanted those stuffed clams. All they had to do was find enough of them and maybe by the end of summer they'd have their bikes. "Okay, let's go," he said, "but we have to be more careful than ever."

Asa grinned as he climbed into the boat. "Get the anchor," he said, and as Ike climbed the muddy bank to retrieve the anchor, Asa picked up an oar and pushed the stern of the boat out into deeper water and started the outboard. Now they were cooking. No more messing around with clams that anybody could find. He aimed the bow upstream, standing now in order to see where the deeper water lay.

He glanced down quickly to make sure he'd put the tool box in as he thought about the shallow water ahead. It was a long row home if they hit bottom and sheared a pin on the propeller. But he had extra shear pins in the tool box and the tools he needed to change the pin.

He looked at Ike's back as he hung over the bow looking for shoals and rocks. Having him so far forward helped by lifting the stern and allowing the motor to run through water where it would normally hit bottom. They were doing it right, just the way they'd been taught and yet ... yet he could not overcome the sudden deep foreboding he felt. He tried to write it off to having disobeyed their parents, but it did not go away. In fact, the farther upcreek they went, the more certain he was that they were making a mistake. There was trouble ahead and he could feel it.

"How's it look, Ike?"

"Okay," Ike called back over his shoulder, turning his head to the side so he didn't have to take his eyes off the bottom. "Just take it slow in case something big pops up."

Asa nodded. "Okay." The key, he thought, was to be ready for whatever might happen. And when you were in a boat it was hard to see ahead, because you couldn't always see down through the water. In fact, as he thought about it, Asa decided that it was never possible to see very far ahead.

Chapter 2

Treacherous Places

At first they made good time, following the channel from bend to bend in the creek, and then suddenly the channel disappeared, and Asa had to tip the motor on its mount to keep the propeller from biting into the bottom.

"Ike, look for deeper water. I can't see from back here."

"Okay." Ike kneeled on the single board of the front seat and then stood up.

Suddenly he waved his left arm. "Go to port!"

Quickly, Asa put the helm over and they skirted a large rock on the bottom.

For a while the bottom lay clear of any obstructions and Ike watched the smooth black mud slip by and he thought about the Fingernails, the series of shallow tidal ponds which lay hidden in the miles of reeds and grasses. At low tide you could wade any one of them as long as you knew where the holes lay. Nasty, bad places, those holes. Dips in the old creek bed that had been left when the creek cut a new channel.

Over time they filled with soft material like rotting reeds and eel grasses, and if you stepped into one you would simply sink down before anyone could help. At least that's what his dad had told him.

He didn't like it up here at all. Even the creek banks disappeared on the high water, and then you had to know where the channels lay or risk getting lost in the reeds. But their fathers never got lost. They simply picked a channel and then poled through the green wall of reeds, the pointed bows of their smoky green, flat-bottomed duck boats sliding easily past and into the open water on the other side. Then they set out great strings of decoys and waited for the migrating flocks of mallards, black ducks, and canvasbacks. And then once their fathers had shot their limits they gave the boys a chance, explaining how to lead the birds and how to judge when they had come into range. So far neither he nor Asa had shot a duck, though he thought this fall they might do better. They'd both grown a good deal in the past year, and judging by their success at hitting baseballs this spring, their coordination had improved considerably.

Ike waved his right hand. "Starboard!" he shouted, and Asa responded quickly, turning the boat abeam of the current, and using the pressure from the flowing water to keep them downstream of the boulder that lay just inches from the surface. Ike looked around, quickly marking a stump on the bank and then a rock on the other bank so he'd be able to find the boulder on the way down. "It looks okay for awhile," he said, and Asa straightened the boat.

They did not shoot for sport alone. The birds helped feed two families, just as the deer did and getting food that way meant their fathers could reduce their risks by not having to fish the winter seas so often, fighting the ice and the dangerous nor'easters. A wet snow could overload a boat and cause it to capsize and sink in a stormy sea if it caught a wave on the beam. Icy decks increased the chance of falling overboard. Maybe if he thought about that more, he'd shoot better.

But to find one of those ponds you had to know where it lay. The grasses and reeds grew eight feet high and the flat featureless marshes stretched for miles and miles and miles. Either in a boat on the creek or walking in the marsh you could not see through the reeds more than a few feet in any direction, and more than one man had lost his way and wandered for days in the reeds, stumbling across the tiny feeder creeks that meandered like worm tracks across the boggy ground. At high tide, when the marsh flooded, walking anywhere became a dangerous affair because you could no longer see the sink holes or the quick-mud potholes. Which was why their parents didn't want them gallivanting around up here, and why they always carried a compass. Still, by keeping to the creek they had no need of the compass, and they did just that, the outboard motor pushing them slowly up the twisting, winding waterway, sweeping around Fingernail Bend and up to the North Flats, which some claimed was the last good clamming ground on the river.

After that the water grew much shallower and they traveled slower and slower, Ike in the bow, pointing which way the channel ran, and Asa picking off landmarks on the bank so he would have some idea how to navigate the creek coming back down.

Now and again Asa or Ike would dip a hand over the side and taste the water, knowing that at some point the land would rise and the water would taste less and less salty until finally it ran fresh. It surprised them to have traveled so far in salt water, especially on a falling tide when the water went back to the sea and any creek more easily ran fresh.

The tide had not reached full low by noon and still they pushed on, cutting back and forth across the creek. Suddenly Ike pointed to the left bank where the reeds thinned. "There's one!" he shouted.

Asa turned the boat, gunned the engine to get up speed, and then shifted into neutral to keep the prop from fouling as they shot through the reeds and into the channel. It was wide, perhaps thirty feet, and for a way the water was a couple of feet deep and then suddenly it went dead shallow.

"Stop! Stop!" Ike shouted, and Asa cut the motor as the bow of the boat ran slowly up onto the muddy bottom and came to a stop.

They tied safety lines to themselves and to the boat and then climbed out and walked through the ankle deep water in all directions, but they could not find a channel. Off to the left, just showing above the reeds, they could see the trees which grew on the High Ground, closer now, but still some distance to the north. Finally, they found a place where the water ran a little deeper, and they pulled the boat off the mud and towed it to where it floated free.

"Tide's got a way to go," Ike said. "Why don't we eat lunch and then start looking."

"Okay with me," Asa said. "The lower the water, the easier it'll be to find the quahogs."

Ike reached into the boat, dropped the anchor overboard, and then climbed aboard. He unwrapped his sandwich and opened his can of soda. "We'll have to be careful," he said as he pointed to the muddy mark on the reeds nearby. "The whole marsh floods when the tide comes in."

"We'll be okay as long as we watch."

"I still think Kidd buried his treasure up here some-where."

"Where would you look?"

"Like I said. On The High Ground."

"What would you look for?"

"I don't know. I never looked for treasure before. A tall tree with some marks on it, a cave maybe."

"I think I'd rather look for big quahogs."

For awhile the boys ate silently, watching the birds, glad as always to be out on the creek. "Ike, what happened that got you into that fight with Mike?"

"Ahhh, he's a creep."

"Okay, he's a creep. He's also a bully, but not many guys get into fights with him."

"He kept calling me skinny so I punched him."

"He's pretty tough."

"You're telling me. Asa, I hit him as hard as I could and nothing happened. I mean, I suckered him and hit him right on the jaw and he just stood there."

"He's still looking for you."

"I hope I see him coming. He doesn't run very fast."

"I'll give you this, Wilson, you got guts, punching a guy that big. He's at least two years older than us."

"I don't like bullies."

"Me either, but I don't think I'd have punched him."

Ike grinned. "I figured if I didn't knock him over, at least I could outrun him, and that's the way it worked out. But I didn't know he was still looking for me."

"Well, he is, and you'd better keep a weather eye turned

for trouble."

Ike stuffed the sandwich bag and his thermos back into his lunch box. "Speaking of trouble, have you seen Ashley since we got out of school?" He grinned.

"Now what brought her into this."

"I thought you were in love with her."

"In love?"

"Well, that's what it looked like at the dance."

"Just 'cause I danced close to her?"

"Close! I thought she was being mauled by a bear!"

Asa laughed. "You jerk ... she just smelled good."

"Really? Like what? Pizza?"

"I'm not telling, Ike. You want to find out, you'll have to get close to a girl ... real close, but I don't think that's gonna happen soon."

"You think I'm scared of girls, don't you, but I'm not. Not a bit. I just haven't found one to suit my fancy."

"Not even Mary Kelly?"

Ike blushed. "Okay, I'll admit it. I like Mary. But she doesn't like me."

"How do you know?"

"I just know."

"Did you ever ask her out?"

"You're nuts, you know that?"

Asa grinned and let it go while they could still laugh. "You ready to dig some monster quahogs?"

"Let's go for it!" Ike waited till Asa had climbed over the side, and when he was standing in the water with his back turned, he raised his head and cut loose, his voice matching the pitch and intensity of a diving hawk, but so loud and so close that Asa instinctively ducked, trying to cover his head, and instead knocked himself in the ear with the handle of his clam rake.

"Gotcha!"

"Don't do that, Ike!" Asa rubbed the side of his head. "You nearly blew my ear drums out."

"Even?"

Asa nodded. "Can we just dig some clams?"

And that's what they did, digging here and there, always finding a few cherry stones and an occasional quahog, and then suddenly every time they pulled a rake through the rich, black mud they could hear the heavy sound the tines made as they scratched across the ridges on a quahog shell. Sometimes the rake only traveled a foot.

"Wow!" Ike shouted as he held one up. "Look at the size of this one!" And then Asa found a spot, and the boys danced and jumped around and dug and dug, though even in their excitement they took the time to wash each clam before dropping it into their wire baskets so they would not have to clean the mud from the boat later.

"I never saw anything like this!" Asa said. "Do you suppose all the Fingernails have clams like this?"

"I don't know," Ike said, "but if they do we can dig here forever. Maybe we can get our mothers to drive us to other towns on the coast so we can hit more restaurants."

"We ought to get the clams tested so we can get a letter from the state. Otherwise they'll think we dug them near a sewer pipe."

"Can we do that?" Ike asked as he set two more huge clams into the basket.

"Sure."

"Will they want to know where we dug them?"

"Probably."

"Then I say we forget about it. If anybody asks we just tell them how stupid we would be to sell them bad clams. And we ask them to sign up for a regular delivery."

"Maybe our dads could get the letter. They're well-known for only selling good fish." Asa topped off the first basket and brought the empty one closer to where they dug. "And I got another idea. I think we can grow mussels under our piers by hanging them on strings or wires."

"Good idea," Ike said, "you think that up on your own?"

"Naw, I read about it."

When they had filled the baskets they stopped digging and explored with their toes, walking slowly along, feeling the big quahogs in the mud everywhere they walked. And then suddenly, just before they reached the pond itself, Asa felt the bottom give way beneath him. "Ike! Ike! I'm sinking!" He flopped himself out as flat as he could but the mud only seemed to suck him down faster. "Grab my rope!"

Ike moved quickly to the side of the boat, grabbed hold of Asa's rope and pulled, but he wasn't strong enough to fight the sucking mud. "I can't pull it! You're stuck too deep!" Without hesitating he jumped into the boat, hauled the anchor, pushed the stern out into the creek, started the engine, and took up the slack in Asa's rope. Even the fifteen horse engine strained against the load, and at first Ike thought it might not work, except that Asa was no longer sinking into the mud. "Kick your feet!" Ike called. "Swim out of it!"

Asa began pumping his legs and as he did the water from the creek began to mix with the mud, loosening the suction, and he could feel the boat pulling him slowly upward and he kicked even harder. With a sudden rush he came loose and the boat shot forward down the creek dragging him along behind, hollering for Ike to stop the boat.

Ike shut off the engine and pulled on the rope, hauling Asa easily through the water. "You okay?" he asked as Asa grabbed onto the gunwale of the boat.

"Yeah, except that my bathing suit's down around my ankles, and I nearly drowned before you stopped the boat."

Ike laughed, as much out of relief as anything. And then he sat on the far side of the boat to balance it as Asa pulled his bathing suit back up and climbed in.

"That was close," Asa said.

"We shouldn't have come."

"I suppose you're right, but look at the other side of it. We got the best clams ever and there's all kinds of clams here. We just have to wear our life vests when we dig and keep the boat closer and keep checking ahead with our clam hooks. There aren't any clams in that quick mud and when we find a place where the clams give out we drive a stake so we know where not to go."

"Were you scared?" Ike asked.

"I've never been so scared in my life. The stuff just sucks you down and down and down, and it happens fast and it's so sticky that you can't pull out. I couldn't even swim out of it. That was smart using the boat, Ike."

"I think we were just lucky, that's what I think."

"No. We were ready and that's what we have to remember. As long as you're ready for something bad to happen, you can save yourself."

"Luck was a part of it, Asa. We were lucky there was enough water to use the motor. I don't know how I would have got you out." He shook his head.

"You could have kedged me out with the boat and the anchor."

"Maybe."

By then the tide had started in and they threw out the anchor, dumped the clams into the live well in the boat, filled it with water, and sat looking out at the creek. "I'll bet," Asa said, "that nobody has dug in here for a hundred years."

"Who do you suppose owns all this?" Ike asked.

"I never thought anybody did," Asa said.

"But somebody must own it."

"I wonder how much it would cost to buy it."

Ike shook his head. "You mean buy the whole marsh?"

"Sure." Suddenly Asa looked up. "Hey, I'll bet I know who owns it. Mrs. Clairborne. That's who my father bought the land from."

"She died just a little while ago. I remember Mom talking about it one night at supper."

For awhile the boys sat silently looking up the creek toward The High Ground. Finally Ike spoke. "With the tide coming in we'll have enough water to go up and look around for Kidd's treasure."

And now, feeling so good about having escaped from the quick mud and having found such a treasure of clams, Asa decided it might be fun. "Sure," he said, "let's go have a look."

Ike looked up, surprised by Asa's willingness. "You're serious?"

"Sure. Maybe it really is there."

Suddenly Ike wasn't so sure he wanted to go. "Why do you think our parents don't want us up here?"

"I always thought it was because of the sinkholes."

"No, I mean, do you think there's some other reason?"

"Like what?"

"I don't know."

Asa grinned. "Jeez, Ike. First you're all pumped about going up there to look around and now you sound like you don't want to go."

"No. I still want to go, I was just thinking that maybe they know something we don't."

"But they told us about the sinkholes, so wouldn't they have told us if there was something else?"

"You know how parents are. 'I don't have to have a reason, Ike, just do what I say'," he said in a high, woman's voice. "And you never know what they mean."

"I don't know what your parents said, but mine only said I wasn't supposed to go beyond Boulder Bend because of the sink holes. They never said anything about The High Ground. And anyway, we could get there by taking the old road."

"I hadn't thought of that." He laughed. "I really hadn't thought of that." He threw his right fist into the air. "Let's do it!"

"All right!"

Ike pulled in the anchor as Asa started the engine and they headed out to the shallows and the main channel.

But as he watched the water slide past, Ike wondered why he felt so uneasy about going up there. What could possibly happen?

Chapter 3

Encounter On The High Ground

Ike shipped the anchor and then, standing in the boat, each of them armed with a pole, they began poling the boat upstream toward The High Ground. The creek had grown much narrower now, the bottom hard and stony, the current much swifter. But the skiff rode easily up over the current, and it took no great effort to move the boat upstream.

"Do you believe in ghosts?" Ike asked.

"No," Asa said.

"Yeah, me neither."

Using ten-foot red cedar poles they pushed the boat around the next bend, driving the poles into the bottom and pushing the boat up through the current, each stroke moving them steadily closer to The High Ground.

"Sometimes," Ike said, "pirates left dead men to guard the treasure."

"You mean like Flint did in *Treasure Island*."

"Sure.

"I never heard of Kidd doing that."

"There was a lot of treasure that nobody found, or if they did they never lived to tell about it. Maybe he did what Flint did, buried the gold and left a body to guard it."

Around the next bend they could see where the creek swept in close to the woods, and they polled harder, keeping the boat in the slack water where the current eddied. In what seemed like no time at all they reached the woods, climbed out, and tied up the boat.

"I think we ought to look for the biggest tree we can find," Ike said.

"How long ago was he supposed to have been here?"

"Around three hundred years."

"I don't know, Ike, maybe we ought to look for a stump."

"Never thought of that. But don't some of the oaks last that long?"

"I think so," Asa said.

"Well, let's take a look. Like Mrs. Spooling said in class all year, nothing ventured, nothing gained." He shook his head and grinned. "I sure got tired of hearing that."

"Me too." Asa chuckled. "But it was pretty funny when she caught you reading a novel inside your social studies book and you looked up and said, 'nothing ventured, nothing gained'."

Ike laughed. "My mom didn't think it was so funny, but I think my dad did, because I never got punished for it. The best part was when she made me write on the board, 'I won't read novels in class again,' and instead I wrote, 'I won't read in class again,' and she never caught it, or at least she never said anything."

"I think Mrs. Spooling is getting kind of old to be teaching. She must be over fifty anyway."

Slowly they climbed up away from the creek and the marsh, pushing through a thick fringe of hemlocks down near the water and then into a more open stand of hardwoods. Still the brush came well above their knees and pushing through it tired them quickly, and in the heat they began to sweat hard, and with no wind to keep them off, the mosquitoes closed in.

Asa stopped, took a bottle of bug dope from his pocket, squirted some in his hand, and rubbed it on. "Here," he said as he tossed the plastic bottle to Ike. "Put it heavy on your legs to keep the ticks off."

"What is this stuff?" Ike asked as he wrinkled his nose at the odor.

"Skin so Soft. It comes from the Avon lady."

"Smells worse than Mrs. Pillbottom."

Smeared with the sweetly scented oil, they began walking again, only now the hill had grown quite steep and they had to climb more than they walked.

"I don't see any stumps," Asa said.

Ike shrugged. "Maybe he piled up some stones, or he might have made some marks on a rock. That's the kind of stuff pirates put on their maps, anyway."

"That's what we need," Asa said. "A map. If we had a map this would be duck soup."

"But we don't, so we'll just have to look."

Halfway up the ridge, Ike turned and looked back the way they had come. "Hey," he said, "Asa, look at that."

Asa turned. From here he could see over the marsh for miles and miles, all the way down to South Ridge and beyond that to King's Point and the ocean.

"You can even see the piers by our houses," Ike said. "I sure wouldn't mind living in a spot like this."

"Nice view," Asa said "But you'd have to dredge about seven miles of creek to get a real boat up here."

Ike ignored the remark. "And look at the Fingernails." Ike pointed toward the sliver-like ponds glinting brightly in the sun. "You can see every one of them from here." Most of them lay to the west of the creek, curved like fingernail parings, tucked down into the reeds and grasses. One by one they marked the location of the ponds by the bends in the creek so they could walk directly to any one of them by following a compass.

Because of the clams, knowing how to reach the ponds quickly had great value, for surely if clams grew in one pond they grew in the others as well.

"I'll bet there's oysters in there too," Ike said. "Do you know how much money we could make this fall when the oyster season opens?"

"We better make a pact never to tell anyone about this," Asa said.

"It may be hard to keep it a secret."

"If somebody asks, just don't answer. It's not lying if you don't say anything."

"Okay, then we agree not to say anything."

Asa held up his right hand. "Swear to it?"

Ike held up his right hand. "I swear."

"I swear," Asa said and they shook hands on it.

"Com'on," Ike said, "let's get to the top."

Slowly they worked their way upward till Ike suddenly stooped down into the brush. Asa followed his example and then crawled forward till he reached Ike's side. "What is it?" he whispered.

"Look," Ike whispered back. "Somebody's here!"

And judging by the size of the garbage pile, Asa thought that whoever had set up this camp had been here for several weeks. A large camouflage tent stood to one side of the clearing, and a large camouflage fly ran some twenty feet from the door of the tent to a folding table. A small gas stove sat on the table and they could see an ice chest just outside the tent. A pick and two shovels had been placed carefully against a tree to keep the handles out of the dirt. Where there had been digging, the fresh dirt looked like mounds made by a giant mole.

"Someone's looking for treasure!" Ike whispered.

"That's what it looks like, all right."

"He's been digging everywhere."

"I wonder if he found it."

"He'd have left if he had."

"Then he must still be here ..."

They hunkered a little lower into the brush at the thought of getting caught spying.

"We'd better get out of here," Asa said.

Ike nodded and they turned and started downhill, crawling along through the brush. They had crawled less than a hundred feet when Ike stopped, thinking he had heard someone behind them. He listened, but he could hear only the soft rustle of Asa crawling along ahead of him. He decided to risk taking a look and he waited till Asa had gotten well ahead of him, and then poked his head up out of the brush just as an enormous white hand grabbed his arm. He let out a holler like a wounded buffalo and jumped to his feet, twisting and slashing out with his other hand and hitting the man squarely in the stomach. Nothing happened, except that his wrist got bent backward and he hoped it wasn't sprained.

"Run Asa! Run!" he shouted and he twisted and turned but the hand held him fast, gripping his arm as if he'd got it caught in a huge pair of vise-grip pliers. Asa didn't answer, and now the woods seemed very quiet except for the sound of his feet thrashing in the dry leaves as he tried to pull himself free.

The man stared at him, his pink eyes like live coals, and a great mass of pure white hair stuck nearly straight out from his head. Ike tried to pull his arm loose. "Let me go! Let me go!" he shouted.

"Well, well, what is Whitey catching for himself now? What are boys doing in such place as this and where these boys are coming from, Whitey asks. But he gets no answer. Even when he asks, he gets no answer." He tightened his grip, turned, and started back toward the tent, Ike stumbling along behind him.

"We didn't mean anything, mister. We just wanted to look around. We didn't know this was your place."

Whitey did not answer, at least not directly, instead he continued to talk to himself as if there were two of him. "Whitey thinks this is more than just simple case of accident. These be spies, he guesses, spies from the Fishbone, come to find out what Whitey has found with his half of the map. Very clever, Whitey, says he."

Out of the brush, on a path, they walked more quickly toward the tent. "What are you going to do to me?" Ike asked, and when he thought of the possibilities he felt as if he might cry, but all that would do was fuddle his thinking, and if ever he needed to think, this was the time. It was even worse than the state spelling bee when he flubbed the last word and wound up second.

"Let go of my arm. You're hurting my arm. What good would I be with a bad arm. But with a good arm I could help you dig for the treasure."

"Ah ha! Right! Whitey is always right. Only spy could be knowing about map and treasure. A Fishbone spy. We'll miss him, though. Skinny he may be, and two diggers is better than one, but nothing can be done about that, Whitey thinks." He stopped and looked around. "At least we have no trouble about what to do with the body. Any hole will do." Suddenly he grabbed Ike's free arm and looked directly into his face. "How will he do the killing? Strangling of his neck? No, Whitey doesn't like stranglings, too much choking and gasping. No, no strangling. Bashing his head in with a rock? Shoot him? No, can't be no shooting here, the sounds will carry so far. What then, Whitey wants to know. No strangling, no shooting, and no knifing because he will scream unless we just cut his throat and ... yes ... cutting of his throat, that is the best way." He let go of one arm and suddenly a long, wicked looking knife appeared in his hand. "Quickly is best, Whitey thinks, for if it is quickly finished there will be no screaming and hurting of Whitey's ears."

"No, please don't kill me. It's stupid to kill me. People will be looking for me. They're sure to check up here because they know we came this way."

"We?" Whitey looked around quickly. "Whitey forgets about other boy. Dumb stupid thing to do."

"He's gone," Ike said. "By now he's already headed downcreek in the boat."

"No. He will be around. Close by. Not deserting his partner. Waiting. But what does he be waiting for? Boys always lose in fights with men. How best is the way to be doing this?" He shook his head, his white hair unaffected by the movement. "Whitey does not like to being confused. It is too confusing. Simple way is best. Kill one, then find other." He drew the knife closer to Ike's throat.

And then Asa leaped out from behind the tent and using a thick pine branch and his best home run swing, broke the branch on Whitey's back. The knife flew out of his hand as he staggered forward, fighting for breath, and Ike shot free as Whitey fell onto his hands and knees, gasping for air.

Ike and Asa ran off through the brush as fast as rabbits with beagles running close behind.

"Did you kill him?" Ike hollered as they ran. "Did you kill him? I think you killed him!" Ike babbled on and on. "Because if you didn't kill him, then he's gonna be chasing us and ... I hope you killed him!"

The growl from the hill top left little doubt that Asa had not killed him, and they ran faster, despite the danger of running over rough ground where rocks and roots lay hidden, waiting to catch a toe. Whitey growled again, swearing and raving, and Ike shot past Asa and ran for the boat with not a single doubt in his mind but what he was being chased by the ghost of Captain Kidd.

Chapter 4

Escape

Down the hill they ran, scrambling along, grabbing smaller trees to keep from going too fast, and then suddenly they broke over the edge of a sharp drop and for several yards they tumbled downhill, regaining their feet only when the land flattened enough to slow their descent. They plunged on, driven by the howls from behind.

"You can't get away! You're trapped!" Whitey shouted, cackling like a witch, and Asa doubled his speed, passing Ike as they scrambled even faster down the hill, jumping over rocks and stumps. And then Ike hooked his foot on a root, landed on his right knee, and went tumbling into the brush, the pain in his knee bringing tears to his eyes. He couldn't run. All he could do was lie rock still, listening to Asa scrambling along through the dried leaves, and then he heard nothing. Dead quiet. Not a sound, not a single solitary — footsteps! Very close, feet crunching in the dried leaves, coming closer and then stopping. He held his breath. Not a bird sang and the breeze toyed with only the very tops of the trees. The mosquitoes closed in and he prayed one wouldn't bite.

But the mosquitoes only hovered. The bug dope! Of course. He'd forgotten. They'd smeared on plenty of bug dope and that would keep the mosquitoes off. The voice startled him so badly he thought his heart would stop.

"Fast these boys is, yes very fast, but not so smart. Bug dope they has on and Whitey can smell that, and he will track them down, and he will kill them, and roast them on a spit like the little pigses they is, who come spying on Whitey."

The footsteps started again, loud at first and then softer and softer as if he were moving away, and Ike waited. The pain in his knee had faded and he didn't think it'd slow him down a whole lot. Nor did he still think Whitey was the ghost of Captain Kidd. Just a crazy man with white hair and pink eyes. An albino. Maybe a zombie. An albino zombie! That did not make him feel the least bit better, except that while you could not outrun a ghost, you could outrun a man and especially you could outrun a zombie, 'cause mostly they just went lurching around ... or at least that's what they did in the movies. The footsteps grew more and more faint.

The quiet that followed seemed almost loud. He waited, and when he heard no sounds, he decided to make a run for it. He climbed up onto his feet, squatting and ready to run, when he remembered a trick from a book he'd read, where a guy pretended he was walking away by making softer and softer footsteps. And then he remembered another trick, one he'd used on Asa. He picked up a rock and threw it way off to the west. The stone crashed through the brush and bounced away down the hill, and Whitey turned and ran off in the direction of the noise. It had been a trick all right, trying to make him think he had left when he hadn't moved. He couldn't have been more than six feet away! Slowly Ike raised his head and peeked through the tops of the underbrush until he could see the white hair flashing in the shafts of sunlight through the trees. Maybe he wasn't a zombie after all, at least not from the way he ran. He crouched to test his knee. It hurt but he moved quickly, without running, keeping low, and using the trees as a screen.

He heard Whitey coming and he headed east to the steep part of the ridge, moving past a gigantic old stump, and dropping down over the rocks while using the ledges for cover, but making enough noise to wake a hibernating bear.

Halfway down he stopped to listen, hearing Whitey crashing through the underbrush and then suddenly at the top of the ridge he stopped. A terrifying cackle sliced through the quiet. "Whitey thanks boys, he does! Yes, he thanks them! Run along home now, run along home! Whitey is not harming boys who help him so!"

Ike looked uphill between the rocks to where Whitey stood on an enormous rotted stump. Whoa, he thought, I led him right to it! But how could I have known it was there? He ducked out of sight and moved on down the ridge, reaching the thick hemlock fringe and cutting through to the marsh and the creek, popping out of the cover just north of where Asa waited.

With the reeds to hide them, they walked through the ankle-deep water to the boat. Still they did not talk, but put on their life jackets and holding the boat by the gunwales, walked it along, keeping to the high reeds, knowing that as long as they could not see the ridge, anyone up there could not see them. When they thought the water ran deep enough to use the engine, they climbed into the boat and Ike kept the bow headed downstream.

Asa uncocked the motor and lowered the shaft but it hit bottom and he cocked it up and then several seconds later tried it again. Still not enough water. The creek began its turn back toward the bank below The High Ground, and the water would run deeper closer to the bank. He pointed that way and Ike stroked the boat closer with his left oar. Asa set the throttle at start then shifted the engine into neutral, praying it would start on the first pull. If they had to row, Whitey could wade out and grab the boat. The only thing to do was pull the starter cord hard enough to spin the flywheel as fast as possible. He stood up and gripped the cord with both hands, and then pulled all at once. The engine roared into life and he dropped into the seat, shifted into forward, and wound the throttle to full speed.

From there to Ike's pier he ran with the throttle on the fifteen horse engine wide open, not caring whether he hit anything. The important thing now was distance, and he wanted to get as far as he could from The High Ground.

At Ike's pier, he swung the boat in against the floating dock and tied up.

"Did you get a good look at him?" Asa asked.

"You should have seen him!" Ike said. "I thought I was seeing a ghost. He's all white. As white as an egret. Hair and eyebrows, and his skin is so white you can see the veins underneath, and his eyes are pink and they glow like they're on fire. And he's very tall and ... Asa, I gotta tell you, the worst nightmare I ever had didn't scare me as much as he did. I think he's an albino, but if somebody told me he was a zombie I'd believe it, even though he runs too fast for a zombie. He talks to himself too, calling himself Whitey. He sounds as crazy as Drunken Donny Dunn down to King's Point."

"Wow! A zombie!"

"At first I thought it was the ghost of Captain Kidd!"

"It can't be," Asa said. "If it was Kidd's ghost he would have known where to dig."

"I didn't think of that. Must be a zombie then."

"Or somebody who knows there really is a treasure buried there somewhere."

Ike shook his head. "He only quit chasing me when he came to the big old stump that we were looking for." Ike shook his head. "And now he'll find the treasure." He sounded as if his parents had forgotten his birthday.

"No wait! Ike, if he was looking for the stump then he must have a map, right?"

"What good does that do us?"

"Maybe we could sneak in and steal the map."

"Are you crazy? I'm not getting anywhere near him. He was going to kill me, Asa! I mean he was going to slit my throat with his knife!" He looked around at Asa, his eyes very wide. "Hey. You saved my life."

"I just wish I'd hit him in the head, and I would've, but I was afraid I'd either miss him or maybe kill him."

"He's crazy and we ought to get the police up there, before somebody gets killed."

"If we do that everybody will know we were there. No. No matter what, we can't tell our parents about this."

"Then we call the police and not tell them who we are. Asa! If anybody goes up there, he'll kill 'em."

"In the first place nobody ever goes up there, and in the

second place, Mrs. Dickerson answers the phone and she'd recognize our voices, but the worst part is that they'd want to know what he was doing up there, and even if he didn't tell them, it wouldn't take long for them to guess."

"Yea ..." Ike looked down at the floor of the boat. "I suppose you're right."

"What was all that talk about spies?"

"He thinks somebody called Fishbone sent us to spy on him, and ..." Ike sat straight up in his seat. "I forgot! He said he had a map! But he's only got half-a-map and this Fishbone guy has the other half."

"What kind of map?"

"What else? He's got Kidd's map."

Asa, looking doubtful, just shook his head.

"Well, what other kind of map would he have? A gas station road map?"

"I don't know what to think." He looked up at the sun. "Suppose I pick you up tomorrow morning at five and we take the clams down to King's Point. Maybe we can go to the library and find out more about Captain Kidd."

"You're thinking about going back there, aren't you?" He shook his head. "If it means going back there, Asa, you're gonna have to count me out."

"But we gotta go, Ike. Now that we know he's there, we can spy on him without any chance of getting caught."

"I'll think about it."

In spite of himself, Asa began to worry. It sure had looked as if the guy had been about to cut Ike's throat, he couldn't deny that, and he supposed if it had been him who almost got his throat cut, he wouldn't be real eager to risk it a second time. "I'll tell you what. After we sell the clams, and after we go to the library, we'll check the wanted posters at the post office. Anybody that looks like that should be easy to spot. Then we can go to the police, okay?"

Anything that delayed going back to The High Ground suited Ike but it got them no closer to finding Kidd's treasure. "Once the cops go up there the rumors'll start."

"But maybe that's okay," Asa said. "If he's doing anything wrong, they'll arrest him."

"The whole town'll go too."

"Maybe, maybe not. Whitey's not gonna tell 'em what he was looking for, and if we say we think he's digging for Indian artifacts, that's what everybody else will think too. Jeez, Ike, nobody but us believes Kidd buried his gold here."

Ike hooked his thumbs into his bathing suit. "If we do go back we ought to take our twenty-two's."

"I know what my Dad will say."

"Well I'm taking my rifle even if I have to sneak it."

"Maybe he isn't doing anything unusual," Asa said.

"Did you see how many holes he's dug? Jeez, Asa, why else would anyone spend all his time digging holes, if it wasn't to look for treasure? And he's crazy. Did you hear that laugh?"

Asa shook his head. He had no answer. "Do you really think he was going to kill you?"

"You saw him, Asa! You saw the knife!"

"I didn't even know he had a knife till you told me."

"You think I'm lying?"

"No. I just don't know whether he was trying to scare us off or whether he was serious."

"I'm telling you, Asa, he was going to kill me and the only thing that saved me was when you hit him with that branch. If you'd been a couple of seconds later he would have slit my throat from ear-to-ear!"

Asa nodded. "We'll have to go back," he said, "and I guess we better bring the rifles." He looked up at Ike standing on the pier.

"There won't be much at the library," Ike said. "I've read every book there that has anything to do with pirates."

"Just a hunch," Asa said. He started the engine and as Ike let go of the gunwale, Asa shouted, "See you in the morning." Then he opened up the motor and headed for home.

The motor was running rough again and he decided that the first thing he was gonna do was put new spark plugs in his engine. After all the years of Dad telling him about maintaining engines, about how you never went out on the water unless you were certain your engine was running perfectly, he couldn't believe he'd forgotten to change the plugs.

His thoughts drifted back to Kidd's treasure. Could it possibly be here somewhere? Or was it just a story that people liked to tell? How could you ever know about stuff like that? How did you know when something wasn't true and when it was? He shook his head and looked toward the point where a line of great boulders ran out into the creek. Even at high tide he gave it a wide berth. But, he wondered, did it matter if what anyone said was true? The real question was whether he believed it. Ike believed the gold was here. Did he? Instead of a nice clear answer, he got something in the middle.

Sometimes. Sometimes he believed the stories and sometimes he didn't, though just now he was leaning more toward believing than not, and he decided that the best way to look at it was just to let things go along and see what turned up ... as long as it had as little as possible to do with Whitey.

Chapter 5

Fishbone

Asa had just finished putting the new spark plugs into his outboard when his father cleared the bend above South Flats and blew the whistle on *The Shitepoke*. Tar, their big black Labrador retriever, leaped to his feet and barked twice, his thick tail sweeping back and forth as he watched the boat making toward the pier.

Asa moved his rowboat around to the side of the pier, tied it up, and then hooked the gas line to the motor. He primed it by squeezing the bulb in the rubber gas line and then pulled the starter cord on the engine. It caught first try and he let it warm up, revving the engine once before letting it idle. It ran like a clock now and he thought maybe next time he might just remember to change the plugs a whole lot sooner. He'd been flat lucky the engine had fired when Ike had needed it to pull him out of the sinkhole. And in fact he'd been lucky again that it fired first try when they were escaping from Whitey.

He shut off the engine and climbed up onto the pier to pet Tar and watch as *The Shitepoke* came steadily up the creek, his father following the channel till he cleared the shallow water at the Flats, and then, riding the high tide, coming straight toward the pier.

The boat was halfway across when he saw a man come out on the afterdeck, make the stern line ready, and walk forward onto the long high bow to uncoil the bow line. What he saw he didn't like; a short, thick man, with a patch over one eye, but a man who knew his way around a boat all right, his short bow legs moving him quickly and easily over the decks of *The Shitepoke* as if he had spent his whole life on that very boat.

Asa watched intently as the forty-foot boat cut through the smooth, glassy water of the creek. The man carried the bow line back to the cockpit and stood by the superstructure of the cabin, holding the line coiled and ready to toss. Why should he not like this man, whoever he was? How could you tell anything by watching him walk about on a boat a half-mile away? It made no sense when you looked at it logically, yet Asa could not deny that from the instant the man had stepped into the open he had felt uneasy.

Not until his father brought the boat up dead in the water alongside the pier and the man leaned out and tossed him the bow line, did Asa see the great scar which ran out from under the eye patch. Never, he thought, had he seen such an evil looking man, yet even with that thought to distract him, he caught the line cleanly and made it fast to the pier as the man, supple and quick as a weasel, stepped from the gunwale to the pier and tied off the stern. Asa stood back, his hand resting on Tar's broad neck, the muscles tense and hard under his hand. He looked down at the dog who was watching the new man closely. And then he was considerably surprised when Tar growled and his hackles rose up under his hand, and Asa could feel his big shoulders bunch beneath his sleek black coat. "Easy, Tar," Asa said. "It's okay, boy."

Tom shut down the engine and stepped out of the cabin. At six-four and broad shouldered as a wrestler, it was easy to see where Asa got his size. "Asa," he called, "this is Fishbone Watson, my new crewman."

The name drove into his brain like an ice pick. Was this who Whitey had meant? Asa nodded, trying not to show the fear that had his heart hammering as if he'd just run a hundred yard dash. "Hi," he said.

"Hello to you," Fishbone said. "From the way you handled that line I'd say you're a pretty fair hand."

Asa forced himself to smile and he knew from the flash in that one black eye, that his hesitation had not gone unnoticed. He tried to cover it. "How was the fishing?"

"Good," Tom said, "in fact with Fishbone to help I had the best day so far this year." He clapped Fishbone on the shoulder as he stepped down onto the pier.

Tar held back, unwilling to pass Fishbone, though he badly wanted to greet Tom as he did every day. Like all Labs, Tar regarded most people as petting machines, but he plainly did not place Fishbone in that category.

"Your dog okay?" Fishbone asked as he looked at the raised hackles.

"What? Tar? He's a pussycat," Tom said. "Best duck dog I ever had. Loves everybody."

Fishbone rubbed the stubble on his chin. "Don't seem to care for me too much," he said. "But then dogs has never took to me, the truth be knowed."

"Tar, down!" Tom said and Tar sat down and his hackles dropped slowly.

Tom nodded and then looked down at the tool box on the pier. "Engine trouble?" he asked.

"Put in new plugs. Runs perfect now."

"Perfectly," his father said.

"Right, perfectly." Asa grinned as he remembered how irritated he used to get when his parents corrected the way he spoke. Now, he was used to it and the corrections didn't bother him, though he'd rather they didn't occur in front of others.

"You and Ike dig any clams?"

"We found a new spot upcreek," Asa said, trying not to make it sound too important, but his father caught the shift in his tone of voice.

"Unless I miss my guess, you boys hit it rich." Tom smiled and turned to Fishbone. "Asa and his pal, Ike Wilson, who lives upcreek a way, know these waters better than anyone around. There's a clam to be found, they'll find it." He turned back to Asa. "Not much of a market just now, though. Every kid in King's Point is digging cherrystones and littlenecks."

"The cook at the Benbow is looking for big quahogs for stuffed clams."

"Just don't keep anything small," Tom said, "Old Smith at the market isn't paying enough to cover your gas."

"I kept some littlenecks for us to eat and some cherrystones for a chowder," Asa said.

Tom looked over the edge of the pier at Asa's boat riding lower in the water than usual. "Why don't you pop down there and open your live wells so we can have a look."

Asa lowered himself carefully into his boat, popped open the covers, reached in, and pulled out a giant of a quahog. "Took all we could get before the tide turned," he said.

Tom grinned. "Now that is a quahog! Look at the size of that thing! Where the devil did you find quahogs that size?" He reached out and took the quahog from Asa, turning it over and over in his hands. "That is one heck of a quahog!"

Asa pretended he hadn't heard the question, hoping it might just slide past, though he knew that was unlikely. Not much got by his father.

"You didn't answer my question."

"What?"

"Where'd you dig 'em?"

"Upcreek."

"Just how far upcreek?"

"A little past Boulder Bend."

Through narrowed eyes Tom tried to evaluate the answer by evaluating his son.

"We found a side creek that doesn't show," Asa said. "Comes in at too sharp an angle. I don't think anybody has ever dug there."

Tom shook his head. "Funny I never noticed it."

"Pretty hard to see," Asa said. "Doesn't look like any other creek."

"You'll have to show me sometime."

"Any time," Asa said, knowing that it wouldn't be any time soon, not at this time of year. There was just too much to get done in a day to spend time searching out a creek. That'd come later when they got closer to duck season. You could never find enough good places to shoot ducks.

"Must be a lot of mud from the dark color," Tom said.

"Sand and mud both," Asa said.

Fishbone chuckled. "Sounds like a right smart young fella you got there, Tom."

"Oh, he's that all right," Tom said. "Hit the crab market just right, netted bunkers before anyone else had found them. Handles a boat good's any man, this one included." He tapped himself on the chest.

They walked off the pier and up toward the house, Asa feeling about as good as a boy can feel when he hears that kind of praise from his father, but his stomach felt empty with fear and his head had gone awash as he tried to figure out a way to tell his father about Fishbone and Whitey without letting on that he and Ike had gone where they'd been told never to go. Even worse he'd lied to his father, and he hated having to do that. It was the worst part of being a kid. Sometimes you had to break the rules, and then you had to lie about breaking the rules, so that every crime was a double crime, and all you could do was feel guilty about it and ... hope you didn't get caught. The problem was that he almost always got caught.

And then another thought occurred to him. Suppose Ike had heard the name wrong? He got pretty scared sometimes and when you're scared you don't always get everything straight. And he'd grant Fishbone Watson this much. He seemed friendly enough, and he smiled a lot, and that made you forget the rough, harsh voice, and the patch, and the long scar that ran halfway down his face. He wondered how his mother would react when she got her first look at Fishbone Watson, for if ever a man looked like a pirate, it was him.

And it wasn't just the patch and the scar either, but something else, a way he had of raising the eyebrow over his good eye and looking at you sideways that made you think he saw more with one eye than most men did with two. It gave him the willies every time Fishbone cocked his head and looked around at him.

As they walked up to the house, nearly a hundred yards uphill from the water, Tar rushed on ahead as always, but now he kept looking back over his shoulder at Fishbone, alert, his body tense and hard looking.

Meg Clark, even when taken by surprise, always hid it well, but then she'd been born and raised in Maine, as had Tom, and circumspection came quite naturally to her. She smiled, shook hands with Fishbone, and invited him in to dinner, all the while making sure Sissy didn't tear the place apart chasing the new kitten from room to room. Tar lay on his rug by the back door, his body hard and ready, his yellow eyes missing nothing.

Little sisters might not be good for much, Asa thought, but she was cute, and he liked the way she got into everything. And she loved to have him play horsey for her, laughing and laughing, and making him laugh until it hurt to breathe. And there was another good part to having a little sister. She took up a lot of Mom's time which meant she had less time to worry about what he was up to. It wasn't as easy for Ike because he had two older sisters so he ended up with three women watching him. What he had to depend on was that they all talked a lot and as soon as they got going, he could slip away without being noticed.

Dinner went well and from the easy, relaxed way his father talked, Asa knew they had caught enough fish to make up for last month. The more he listened to Fishbone, the less he noticed the way he looked, and the more certain he was that Ike had got the name wrong. He had lots of funny stories to tell and he had a fine way of telling them that always made you laugh.

By the time they'd finished the coffee and his father had taken Fishbone down to the cabin, Asa found himself pretty well convinced that his father had found as good a crewman as he could have hoped to find. But even with that, he could not shake the uneasiness he had felt as he stood on the pier watching Fishbone clear the lines. He tried to tell himself there was nothing to worry about. He was only reacting to their narrow escape on The High Ground.

And now, with that so far behind him, it was hard to believe they had been in any danger. Whitey probably wasn't any more dangerous than Fishbone. He'd only been trying to scare us off. Just my imagination working overtime. On the other hand, he must have thought Ike was in some kind of danger or he wouldn't have hit Whitey with that branch. And there was also the matter of Tar and the way he had reacted to Fishbone. Heck, he didn't react that way even when the propane man came, and he hated that guy. It left him wondering whether you could fool a dog.

Chapter 6

The Backswimmer

While his mother put Sissy to bed, he began washing the dishes just as he did every night. He had other chores, like caring for the chickens and keeping the weeds down in the garden, but beyond that he came and went as he pleased, only having to let his folks know where he went and when he expected to get home.

His mother got back to the kitchen just as he started on the pots. "Your father tells me you and Ike had quite a day digging clams," she said.

"Mom, me'n Ike found a ..."

"Ike and I ..." she corrected him.

He grinned. "We found the best quahog bed on the creek. Nothing but giants. You oughta see 'em, Mom, they're huge!"

"How come you didn't tell me before?"

"Had to put new plugs in my engine and then Dad came home with Fishbone, and I guess I forgot." He had forgotten all right, but not because of the engine. It was because of what had happened on The High Ground, and suddenly that all came back as clearly as if he were still there and yet it seemed as distant now as a nightmare in the morning. "The cook at the Benbow says he'll pay double for big quahogs so he can make stuffed clams."

"Are you taking the clams into King's Point tomorrow?"

"Sure. They're nice and fresh."

"You know sometime we'll have to go into town to see about some new school clothes, and maybe after you sell the clams, we ..."

"What's wrong with the clothes I've got?"

"Not only are they worn out, Asa, but they're way too small."

"Gee, Mom, that could take most of a day, and the summer's nearly over."

She laughed, a lovely, high bright sound that always made him smile. "Asa, it's only July."

"I know, but me'n ... Ike — I mean, Ike and I have got a lot of things left to do that we haven't even started on."

"Well, maybe we could do it later. But maybe we could make it on a day when you're going down to sell some clams, and Missy and I will drive in and meet you at Everson's." She finished drying the plates and began on the silverware. "Better yet, I'll call Millie and maybe Ike can get his clothes at the same time."

He sighed. "Okay, but not tomorrow, because Ike and I have some stuff to look up at the library, and we'll probably be there a long time."

"Not tomorrow then," Meg said. "But soon, Asa. I don't want to rush the way we did last year."

"But not too soon because I'll probably grow more by the end of summer and by then the clothes won't fit."

"You won't grow that much."

"I dunno, Mom, I'm growing pretty fast..."

"And you hate shopping for clothes." She smiled. "It's not the end of the world, you know."

"On a rainy day?"

She laughed again. "It's a deal."

Once they had finished cleaning the kitchen, Asa went up to bed. He liked, on warm summer nights, to lie with his windows open, listening to the katydids and the crickets singing about summer. Every day now, memories of the school year grew faded. Not that he didn't like school, but it got in the way of all the other things he wanted to do. He lay with his hands beneath his head, staring up through the dark of the room at the ceiling as a thought he had been avoiding suddenly popped into his mind. High school. This fall he started high school. What would it be like? How much crap would he have to take from the older boys? Jeesh! As if he didn't have enough on his mind. He drove the thought away, telling himself that he'd have plenty of time to worry about that later. For now he had the creek and Ike and ... and Whitey and Fishbone ...

He heard Dad downstairs, opening a beer as he sat at the table with Mom, and almost at once he began to listen closely, for their voices seemed tense and strained, and he got out of bed and lay on the floor, his ear close to where the heat pipe came up.

"I agree," his mother said, "he seems perfectly nice, but there is something about him I just don't trust."

"Meg, he's the best hand I ever hired. He does the work

of two men and he never complains. During a tow when there was nothing to do but keep the tension on the drag, he sat in the wheelhouse and smoked his cob pipe and talked about the places he'd fished, and you heard him tonight. Man's got a gift for the funny story."

"So he has," Meg said.

"I admit his looks put me off at first too, but he works like a demon and he knows how to fish."

"It's more than that," she said.

It made the hair stand up on the back of his neck. So she had felt it too, something dark and sinister, like a rock waiting just under the water to slice open the hull of your boat.

"I don't like his voice," she said. "I think he's seen too much of the bad side of this life."

"That's only 'cause he got a fish bone stuck in his throat once and it damaged his vocal cords."

"None the less, I'd be careful, Tom. Any man that's seen as much as he has is bound to be dangerous. I know I'll not turn my back on him."

Asa slipped back into bed and pulled the covers to his chin, rolling onto his side, wishing he had not overheard his parents talking about Fishbone. Only in the movies had he seen anyone who looked like a pirate, and now he had one living here. And maybe he was nothing more than a fisherman. He certainly handled himself well on a boat, but Mom was right. He shivered once and pulled the covers up over his head. And what if Ike wasn't wrong?

He made himself think about going upcreek for quahogs and how much fun it would be to poke around in all the small side creeks and channels. He thought they might find some long necks too, and maybe even an oyster bed or a mussel shoal. And then he thought again about starting a mussel farm. Maybe he could find some information in the library about how mussels reproduced so he would know how to get started. He'd need to know that and what time of year was best, but he thought they could start by just gathering all the mussels they could find and putting them under the piers. He wondered how you got them to hang onto the strings? Clearly he had a few things to find out but that wouldn't be hard. And whatever it took it'd be worth it. If they could build a supply of big mussels they could count on steady income.

Slowly, buried under his covers, Asa drifted off to sleep. His mother came in to check on him and pulled the covers back so he could breathe more easily, and then turned off his light and went to bed.

He had slept several hours with hardly a dream when suddenly he sat straight up in bed, staring through the dark and holding his breath so he could hear better. Oarlocks. No question about it, you couldn't miss that familiar squeak. He climbed from bed and walked to the open window, staring off into the dark. Down below, in the kitchen, he heard Tar growl and head into the living room where he could stand with his forepaws on the window ledge and look out toward the creek. In the pale, faint light from the quarter moon he saw a boat come quietly around the point and down the creek, a lone man rowing steadily, the outboard cocked up out of the water. And though it seemed odd to see someone on the creek at night, it had happened often enough before when men from King's Point came up after eels for bait. But those men never rowed. They ran their engines. The only time anyone ever rowed was when their motor had broken down.

He rested his cheek on his hands folded on the window-sill as he watched. Whoever it might be, he rowed wonder-fully well, each powerful sweep of the oars driving the boat over the incoming tide. Maybe he'd sheared a pin on the motor or maybe he'd run out of gas and that's why he rowed. In the moonlight the boat with its lone oarsman looked like a giant backswimmer beetle rowing itself along upside down. Water wasps, his father called them, because of the way they could bite. Once he had seen a backswimmer attack and kill a tadpole a hundred times its size.

Just then the boat turned and came diagonally downcreek toward their pier. His eyes grew very wide. It was his boat! Someone had taken his boat and gone off up creek! But who? He watched the boat come in against the pier and saw the man tie it up and then lift two heavy buckets up onto the pier. Only when the man stood did he recognize Fishbone. Asa watched him stretch his arms above his head the way any man would who had spent time sitting in a boat with no seat backs, and then Fishbone picked up the pails, carried them over to *The Shitepoke*, and stepped up over the low gunwale near the stern.

The boat concealed his silhouette, but Asa heard the top go up on the live bait well and then the sound of water being dipped from the creek to fill the well.

Maybe he ought to wake his father, but the more he thought about it, the more certain he grew that Fishbone had just borrowed the boat to go up creek after eels. He hadn't run the motor because he hadn't wanted to wake anyone. And he certainly wasn't sneaking around, Asa thought, as he watched Fishbone walk off the pier and up to the cabin. Tar suddenly began barking and he heard his father get up, walk into the living room, and stop at the window. "It's okay, boy," he said. "Just Fishbone coming back from getting eels."

Downstairs the clock began striking and Asa counted each chime. Ten o'clock. He climbed back into bed, deciding that all his worries about Fishbone amounted to nothing. He made a promise to keep himself under better control. It was always a mistake, he thought, to get too excited over something like the way a person looked. Better to wait and see how he acted. Still, he thought it strange that Fishbone had gone up creek when he had to row against the tide. You could always get eels just below the flats, and if he had gone out at eight he could have rowed on the slack water one way and had the incoming tide to carry him back. It seemed like a lot of extra work. But why row at all? The engine ran like a top with the new plugs.

He climbed back into bed and turned onto his side. Fishbone Watson. Fishbone Watson. Fishbone! Whitey and Fishbone ... Fishbone. If it was the same man, then he must have the other half of the map Whitey had talked about. He climbed out of bed and looked out the window. The lights were still on in the cabin, and he stripped off his pajamas and put on his clothes, and walking barefoot, slipped downstairs and out into the dark night. He crossed the lawn, keeping to the trees and coming up on the cabin in the shadows cast by the birches. The window, because of the way the cabin had been built on piers, was too high, and he slipped around to the back where they kept some extra lobster pots and carried one to the window. He stood on the pot, moving slowly, to keep from making any sound, and then eased himself up alongside the window so he could peek in without showing much of his face.

Fishbone sat at the table in the center of the room, his wide forearms laid flat against the table, his face and his bad eye toward the window as he stared down at a piece of paper on the table.

Asa could not see what was written on the paper, so he stood on his tiptoes, stretching to make himself as tall as possible. That allowed him to see not only that the paper had been torn in half, but that it appeared to be some sort of map. The other half of Whitey's map! It had to be.

He tried to inch just a little higher and just then the old lobster pot tipped to one side and he fell, hitting the ground with a solid thump, and then he took off running as fast as he could run, even as he heard Fishbone curse and throw open the cabin door, slamming it against the wall. Asa dropped to the ground, lying huddled in the birches, his dark clothes his only protection. He kept his face down in the deep grass and listened.

"Who's there?" Fishbone said. "Is that you, Whitey? What the devil are you doing creeping around in the dark?"

For a minute or so it was quiet. Then he heard Fishbone pick up the old lobster pot and drop it. Another curse. "If you can hear me, Whitey, don't get any funny ideas. You know what happened the last time you crossed me."

He heard him walk back to the cabin and stomp up onto the porch. He heard the door bang shut and slowly he raised his head. But he dared not run. The light still burned in the cabin, but he couldn't tell whether Fishbone was inside or not. He thought perhaps it was a trick, slamming the door to make him think he'd gone inside when all the time he was waiting outside in the dark for someone to make a sound he could hear.

His clothes were wet now, soaked through by the dew and he could feel the cold beginning to eat into him, and he wanted to be back in his warm bed, safe in the house, but he ground his teeth together and waited. He tried to take his mind off the cold by thinking about things that were warm, but in the end he simply said to himself, it's summer and the only reason I feel the cold is because I'm wet, and I've been a lot colder and wetter than this before. If I have to lie here all night, then that's what I have to do.

He had no choice. He had to assume that Fishbone was every bit as dangerous as Whitey, and probably a whole lot trickier. His only advantage lay in being patient. But until then he had never thought of himself as patient. He tried to keep track of time by counting, but he tired of that quickly and with every passing second it grew harder and harder to lie there.

He did not know how long he waited, but suddenly he saw a figure on the porch, just a silhouette against the silvery light that ricocheted from the creek. Slowly the figure turned, and Asa heard the door squeak as it opened and closed. Seconds later he saw a shadow pass through the light in the cabin. Slowly, he made his way back into the trees, slipping around to the far side of the house and inside.

He closed the door and turned the deadbolt, something they never did, but he knew he would not sleep with the door unlocked. Finally, he climbed out of his damp clothes and hung them carefully over the chair to dry. Wet clothes in the morning would only raise a lot of questions when he got back from King's Point. And right now he didn't need any more questions, though he was pretty sure that's about all he'd find for some time to come.

Chapter 7

Ike's Bad Dream

Ike lay in bed reading once again the chapter in his pirate book on Captain William Kidd. He hadn't been much of a pirate. In three years of sailing the *Adventure* off Africa he had taken only one big prize, the *Quedagh Merchant,* which carried gold, silks, saltpeter, and pig iron. Then he'd sailed for home, and somewhere along the coast of North America he sold both his prize and the *Adventure* and bought a small three-masted sloop-of-war. He buried part of the gold on Gardiner's Island off the end of Long Island and then sailed north toward Boston. The Gardiner family had found the gold he buried there, but most of it had never been recovered. Some books said he stopped in Connecticut and then on Cape Cod, but no book that he'd read said Kidd had stopped here. And yet there was certainly a reason why the people who lived here then had named it Kidd's Creek. The oldest map he'd seen called it that, though he could not remember now whether he had ever seen a map dated before 1700. Why? Somebody must have made one. Somewhere he was sure there was proof that Kidd had sailed up this creek. But where?

And there were other questions too. Why had he bought the sloop? Speed? Surely it was a faster ship. But what else? Draft? It would have drawn a lot less water than the *Adventure,* he thought. Why had he wanted a faster, shallow draft ship? For coastal work, dodging in and out of creeks and shallow bays where the British couldn't follow with their enormous ships of the line? Could he have sailed such a ship up Kidd's Creek?

He finished reading the section on Kidd which ended with the pirate being hanged in England. The only question, Ike thought, as he set the book on his night table and turned off the light, was whether Kidd had really ever sailed up Kidd's Creek.

He closed his eyes. Maybe tomorrow they could find out more about ships and how much water they drew and how much cargo they could carry. Miss Jameson, who ran the library, could find a book on anything, and though he'd read every book she had on pirates he had never looked into books on sailing ships.

He rolled onto his side and closed his eyes and instantly the vision he had spent the rest of the day trying to chase away, exploded into his mind. Whitey, Whitey and his long, long knife. If it hadn't been for Asa he'd be dead. Good old Asa, strong as an ox, the toughest kid in school even when you counted in the high school guys. Nobody messed with Asa, and mostly because he and Asa were the best of friends, nobody messed with him. Except Mike. Mike wanted to get into a fight with Asa, but Asa wouldn't fight him. And that struck him as strange. Asa never ducked a fight. Why wouldn't he fight Mike? But come to think of it, none of the other guys fought Mike either, not even some of the big kids, who could have beaten him up easily. He started to doze and then suddenly he came awake again.

What if Whitey came looking for them? But wouldn't that be a dumb thing to do? For sure he didn't want trouble, but if I were him, Ike thought, wouldn't I expect it after having tried to kill someone? Wouldn't that kid be likely to tell his parents and wouldn't the parents call the police? And he couldn't know that he and Asa had been forbidden to go that far upcreek. And who was Fishbone? The questions whirled in his head, and he thought if only he could find some answers he would feel much, much better.

The thing that terrified him most was the thought of going back up there, and yet he had to go because Asa was going and he couldn't let him go alone. How could anyone be that brave? But then Asa had always been like that, always willing to take a risk. Yet as he thought about it, he realized that while he took risks, Asa never took chances. He never took a dare, and he was careful, and he thought ahead. And now , even just knowing Whitey was there made a big difference, and knowing that he didn't see very well gave them a clear advantage.

What it came down to was that Kidd's treasure was at stake. If he brought his twenty-two they could at least defend themselves, and he didn't think Whitey would guess they'd be armed.

Suddenly he wondered whether his dad had locked the doors. Dumb question. They never locked the doors. He turned back the covers, and creeping quietly as he could, went downstairs, locked the back door, tiptoed into the living room, and locked the front door.

With that done he felt much better, and then he remembered the dogs. If anyone came near the house the hounds would start howling from their pen. Nothing could creep up without running afoul of Barney and Doris. He rolled onto his side again and then onto his stomach. Kidd's treasure ... was it really there? Was there really a map? He thought about the red Honda dirt bike at Bousquet's and how neat it would be to make their own track, and then as thought connected to thought he finally fell asleep.

The dream began with him sitting in the bow of the boat where he always sat when Asa ran the engine. They had traveled well past Boulder Bend, headed for The High Ground, gliding easily along, the bow of the boat shearing through the smooth clear water in the creek, the wake behind a double line of fading foam. The tide had risen high enough so they did not have to follow the channel, and by cutting the corners they saved a lot of time. And then as they came round East Hook, cutting yet another corner, a huge flock of snowy egrets leaped into the air. There must have been a thousand birds, he thought, and they flew very low over the boat, small white feathers falling like snowflakes, and then the birds wheeled in the sky and came toward them again, just above the water this time, stabbing out with their long, black bills as they passed over, forcing them onto the floor of the boat. And then the birds rose upward and flew out over the marsh, their calls clattering back as they faded into the distance.

Asa gunned the engine and the boat shot forward, the breeze from their passage sucking the small, white feathers from the boat and from their clothes, and leaving a trail like snowflakes bobbing in the wake.

"I never saw so many at one time," Asa said. "They must have a nesting ground nearby."

"They wanted to kill us," Ike said. "They were pecking at us just like they do at the minnows." He shook his head. "We better go back."

"Naw," Asa said. "We just scared them, that's all. They're gone now." He brushed the few remaining feathers from his hair. "If they had wanted to stab us they could have. They just wanted to scare us away."

"But why? There's no rookery around here. Why would they attack us like that?"

Asa shrugged. "At least they're gone."

And then suddenly a giant white vulture the size of a full grown man flew up from the reeds.

"Turn back, Asa, turn back!" Ike shouted, but Asa would not turn. And the giant white bird circled lower, staying directly above the boat. It followed them around Fingernail Bend and between there and the North Flats, it twice swept almost within reach, before rising up to circle once again.

They rounded the turn past the North Flats and the water grew shallow, though the tide had risen enough to keep the motor from hitting, and then suddenly the bird let out a great screech and dove straight at them. Asa turned the boat first one way and then the other, but the bird could not be fooled, turning and twisting in the air as it matched each evasive maneuver. It's pink albino eyes glinted in the bright light as they fixed on him.

"Jump!" Asa shouted as he turned off the engine. "Jump, Ike, jump!" he shouted again as he dove over the side.

Ike stood to jump and just then the bird lowered its talons, caught him by the back of his shirt, and lifted him away, pumping its wings as it climbed higher and higher. Asa scrambled back into the boat and pulled his rifle from under the seat. He pumped a shell into the chamber and aimed at the huge bird, sighting carefully and then squeezing back on the trigger. The twenty-two cracked and he pumped in another round and fired again, and suddenly the bird let go and Ike fell toward the water, turning in the air ... falling ... falling ... falling ...

And then he woke up, lying on his back, his face covered with sweat, panting as if he had been running a race. He wanted to rub his eyes, to make sure he had escaped from the dream, but he dared not pull his arms from beneath the covers, and the dream stuck to his mind, refusing to let go. He began to shake as if he had fever chills. And then his light came on.

"Ike? Are you all right?" his mother asked.

"I ... I gggguess ssoo," he said.

She walked over and sat on the edge of his bed. "You must have had some bad dream," she said, "but that's all it was." She brushed back his short, blond hair. "You're soaked," she said. "Let me get you some fresh pajamas." She walked to his dresser, took out a clean pair, laid them on the bed, and turned on his bedside lamp. "You get into those and I'll get you a nice glass of milk to help you sleep."

"Okay," he said, but after she left the room he still did not dare move. Finally, when he heard the familiar sounds of her moving about in the kitchen, he began to relax. He listened for the dogs, but they were quiet. He held his breath as he listened for other sounds but he could hear only his mother in the kitchen below. Finally he worked up the courage to climb out of bed and change into the nice dry pajamas. He slipped under the covers as his mother came back with the milk.

"Here," she said. "This will help."

He sat up, drank the milk, and handed her the glass. "It's okay," he said. "It was just a bad dream."

"Must've been a doozy," Millie Wilson said. "You hollered so loud you woke your father and not even a hurricane can do that." She smiled down at him, bent over, kissed him on the forehead, and smoothed his hair. "You want me to stay for a few minutes?"

"No, Mom, I'm okay now. Thanks," he said.

"S'what moms are for," she said.

"Can I leave my light on?"

"Course you can. I'll just turn off the top light."

"Thanks," he said.

He lay on his back for awhile, thinking about the dream. It was a pretty dumb dream, he thought. You never saw snowy egrets in flocks, and there was no vulture the size of the one in his dream, and he had never heard of an albino vulture. But one thing was sure. He was taking his rifle with him when they went back up to The High Ground.

Chapter 8

A Surprise At The Library

Ike caught the line and hadn't even had time to tie up the boat before Asa had shut off the engine and scrambled out onto the pier and started talking.

"Wait till I tell you! You won't believe it! The Fishbone, the guy Whitey called The Fishbone. His name is Fishbone Watson and Dad just hired him on as a hand!"

"You're kidding!"

"God as my witness, he's living in the cabin, and last night I crept down there and looked through the window and he was looking at a map that had been torn in half. I couldn't get a real good look so I stood on a lobster pot, and when I tried to get a little higher, the lobster pot went out from under my feet, and I fell and he chased me, and he must have thought I was Whitey 'cause he called his name and he said, 'you know what happened the last time you thought to cross me'."

Ike held the painter from the bow of the boat, the rope looped around a piling. "You're sure about this?"

"Of course I'm sure, you idiot! I just told you what happened. Everything fits. They have a map and what else could they be looking for but Kidd's treasure?"

"We gotta be real careful, Asa, these guys are killers."

"If you think Whitey is scary, wait'll you get a load of Fishbone. He looks like a pirate. Even has a patch over one eye and a huge scar that runs halfway down his face, and he talks with a nasty scratchy sound because of getting a fish bone stuck in his throat once."

"We gotta think this through, Asa. We gotta have a plan."

"I think from what Whitey said and what Fishbone said, they used to be partners and just now they're not. I think Whitey's trying to get all the treasure for himself only Fishbone doesn't know that yet. And last night Fishbone went upcreek for eels, and I don't know how long he was gone and ... Hey!" He looked down at the gas tank on the floor near the stern. "Look at that. I filled it yesterday when I got home and now there's only half-a-tank! He couldn't have used that much gas just to go eeling. He must have set the eel pots and then gone upcreek, looking for Whitey."

"But we're going downcreek, right?"

"Yeah, now we are. The clams are nice and fresh and we need to go see Miss Jameson."

"Okay. That's okay. But going back up to The High Ground until we know just what we're going to do would be nuts."

"Sure it would. We gotta figure this whole thing out first."

Ike tossed the painter into the boat and climbed down.

The bow, from the pressure of the current, swung out toward the open water and Asa started the engine. From there until they reached King's Point they sat quietly, the roar of the engine preventing any talk unless they shouted. Voices carry very well over water, and what they wanted to talk about, they did not want anyone to hear.

A half hour before the library opened, Asa and Ike had sold every quahog for double what the fish market would have paid when prices had peaked. And having topped up the gas tank, they sat in the boat eating jelly doughnuts and sharing a quart of milk.

"Boy I had an awful dream last night," Ike said. "All about a giant albino vulture that tried to carry me off. You were in the dream too." He bit into a fat doughnut, catching the jelly in his hand as it squirted out the side. "You shot the bird with my twenty-two and it dropped me, and then I was falling and falling."

"What happened?"

"I woke up."

"I hate bad dreams," Asa said. "I think about 'em for days."

"Me too." Ike picked the quart milk carton from the seat. "I'm not going up there again without my rifle."

"There was something else I didn't tell you about Fishbone."

Ike's eyes grew very wide and they shown bright green in the morning light. "What?"

"When Fishbone came back down the creek in my boat he was rowing against the tide like he didn't want anyone to know where he'd gone. I figure Dad told him to go downcreek to the big eeling grounds, but he went upcreek instead because he had something else on his mind, like whether Whitey was up there somewhere."

"Maybe he and Whitey *are* working together."

Asa bit into another doughnut. "But then why would he go to work for my father instead of just going up there and digging?"

"Doesn't make much sense, does it."

Asa shook his head. "I wonder which way they tore the map."

"That big stump must be on Whitey's half. Maybe that'll lead him to the treasure."

"Maybe," Asa said. "But suppose that big tree was used to sight to something else. And most likely that something else is on the other half of the map. Maybe Kidd didn't bury anything on The High Ground."

"I wish we could talk to our fathers about this. Nobody knows the marshes the way they do."

"But we can't. First we're forbidden to go up there and second, they won't believe us anyway."

"Why wouldn't they believe us?"

"You know why."

"You mean last summer when we thought we'd found that Indian burial ground and they wasted a whole day to find out that all we'd found was an old family graveyard that nobody knew about."

"That's why."

"But there is an Indian burial ground around here some-where. All the old maps say it's up on The High Ground," Ike said. "Maybe that's all these guys are looking for. Muse-ums pay a lot for good relics. And we know the Indians had a main camp there, so it stands to reason it'd be a good place to dig. If he had found a lot of good stuff, he'd want to scare us badly enough to make sure we didn't come sneaking back when he was sleeping. It's against the law to remove relics anymore."

"Maybe, but then why would he have got so excited about finding the stump?" He looked into the doughnut bag. "Hey, how many doughnuts did you eat?"

"Just my share. There should be two left for you."

Asa looked into the bag. Two. He should have known better than to accuse Ike of anything like that. "Sorry," he said, "I didn't see the other one."

He finished the doughnuts and milk, and they climbed out of the boat and walked up through the village, taking a shortcut over Wolf Fish Lane. As they walked up the narrow street, the tattered sign for The Eelpot hung out over the sidewalk ahead of them. No place in town had a reputation like the Eelpot, Asa thought. The roughest men around went in there to drink, and once a night Mountain Mike, the owner, had to break up a fight. Men had even been killed in there. But the fishermen all stopped from time to time to discuss the fishing and politics, and to look for crewmen. It was where his father had found Fishbone.

"Maybe we oughta ask Mountain Mike," Asa said. "He knows about all kinds of things, and that's where Dad met Fishbone."

"You mean just ... walk into the Eelpot!" Ike stopped. "You're crazy, Asa, that place is full of all kinds of drifters and riffraff."

"As long as we say who we are, I think it'd be okay," Asa said.

"If my mom ever found out, I'd be grounded for the rest

of the summer."

"Okay," Asa said. For a second he thought to tease him about it, to say something like 'well, if you're afraid ...' But that would only have hurt Ike's feelings, and anyway, Ike wasn't afraid of much. Not only that, but it just wasn't the kind of thing you did to your best friend.

They walked past the Eelpot. "You still thinking of going to the cops?" Ike asked as they turned away from the waterfront.

"I think it's worth trying."

"I don't know, Asa, maybe it'll make him madder."

"But if he's trespassing, they have to arrest him, and then he's out of there, at least for awhile."

"It reminds me of poking a hornet's nest."

Asa grinned. "Done that a few times."

"And got stung too."

"If you don't want me to do it, I won't, but we can't go back up there with our rifles. The thing is, Ike, we can't kill him. We'd go to jail."

Ike looked down the street toward the police station. "You gonna tell them about what happened?"

"I was gonna see how it went, but I don't think so. It'd get too complicated."

Ike stopped. "Your hunch about the quahogs was right, so maybe this one is too."

"Ike, if you don't want me to, I won't."

"No. I think you better follow your hunch. You're pretty good at hunches."

They walked up the steps and pushed through into the office.

"Well," Mr. Caruthers said as he looked up from his desk.

"What brings you young fellas around?"

"We wanted to tell you about a guy we saw up on The High Ground."

"Know all about him. Digging for artifacts. Harry Clairborne give him permission." He pushed back from his desk and walked over to the counter. "Clears up one thing, though. He come in here saying people was trespassing up there, and I guess that must have been you two young explorers. Said he was worried about people stealing the stuff he'd found."

"Land's not posted," Ike said. "How could we have been trespassing."

Mr. Caruthers smiled. "S'what I told that fella. Can't trespass on land that isn't posted. Still, it'd be best, I think, you just stayed clear of there till he's finished and gone." His expression changed and a frown drew his eyebrows in toward his nose. "Not a very friendly fella."

"So we noticed," Asa said. "Chased us half-a mile."

"We thought maybe somebody had escaped from the State Hospital," Ike said.

Mr. Caruthers smiled. "Didn't care much for him myself. Be best you just give him a wide berth."

"We will," Asa said. "It just seemed a little strange."

Mr. Caruthers nodded. "What were you boys doing so far upcreek, anyways?"

Ike grinned. "It's summer vacation, Mr. Caruthers. We were exploring."

"Looking for Captain Kidd's old treasure, I'll bet."

"What else?" Ike said.

"Well, good luck to you. Been a lot of folks tried that over the years. Nothing been found yet." His eyes seemed to take on a distant quality as if he were remembering something from a long time ago. "Nice way to spend a summer," he said.

Asa grinned. "Pretty exciting."

"Just stay away from The High Ground. That fella doesn't care for any company."

"We will," Ike said.

Outside, headed for the library, Ike turned to Asa. "Well, what do you make of that?"

"I think that Whitey's smarter than we gave him credit for. Even if we'd said anything about the knife, they wouldn't have believed us. Adults never believe a kid's word against an adult's."

"Pretty dumb, if you ask me," Ike said. "I mean how could anybody ever believe someone who looked like Whitey?" He shook his head. "If ever a man looked like he ought to be in jail, it's him."

Asa shrugged. "Wait till you see Fishbone Watson."

They turned at the end of the street and walked along the shoulder of the road in the shade of the big old sugar maples without talking.

Miss Jameson, a thin woman in her late forties, with her graying hair pulled into a tight bun at the back of her head, sat at the desk smiling as she always did when her better customers came in. And both Ike and Asa took out a lot of books.

"Well, well," Miss Jameson said. "Two of my best readers. What are you looking for today?"

Ike grinned. "We want to know whether Captain Kidd really did sail up the creek. Are there any books or anything else that might mention that, Miss Jameson?"

She adjusted her glasses and then stood. "It's not in a book, exactly, but I have got something." They waited as she stepped out from behind her desk. "Follow me," she said, and they walked behind her to the basement door, and then down the old wooden stairs where they had not gone before. "What I have is a diary and some old maps which were recently donated to the Historical Society. We hold such things here for safekeeping. I can't let you stay down here, but we'll take them upstairs and you can sit at a table."

She walked down an aisle filled with boxes of papers and rows of old, dusty looking books till she reached the end. She took a book from the shelf, opened the cover to make sure she had the right one and closed it. Then she picked a flat, folded piece of paper from the shelf above. "This all came in just two weeks ago after Mrs. Clairborne died," she said as she pointed to several cartons. "She left them to the Society, and when I was making a list of everything, I came across this diary and the map. I've only read parts of the diary, but I think it may tell you what you want to know."

They started back toward the stairs. "This was written around 1700 by Josiah Thompson. He lived on the Creek and he wrote about what happened. No one now is sure just where he lived, but there's a foundation hole in the woods near your house, Ike, and some rotted piles in the creek and most people think that was Josiah Thompson's place."

"Each entry has a date," Miss Jameson said, "and you want to read the entries for August of 1700. If you have any questions, I'll be at my desk."

"Thanks," Ike said.

"Yeah, thanks a lot, Miss Jameson," Asa added.

"I think you'll find it very interesting reading. And one other thing. Nobody but me has read this book for years and years. It was in a box of old books, and I found it way down at the bottom. I don't think Mrs. Clairborne even knew she had it." She smiled. "Of course nobody can say whether any of it's true, but I do know that the old timers didn't spend a lot of time making up stories and writing them down. Writing was much harder work in those days. It took a lot of time having to keep dipping a quill in ink." She smoothed the front of her dress. "I was going to call the newspaper about this and I would have if Mr. Springer had ever printed anything nice about the library."

At the top of the stairs she let them pass and then turned off the lights and closed the door. "Now this diary is very, very old and some of the writing is hard to read." She set the book on the table and Ike and Asa sat down as she went back to her desk and brought them a stack of paper and a pencil. Carefully she drew several letters on the top sheet of paper. "This is the way they used to make some of their letters," she said, "and you'll need to know that to read the diary. And you have to be very, very careful, because this book cannot be replaced. I hope to make a copy of it as soon as the Library Board and the Historical Society give me the money, but I see no harm in letting you read it." She smiled. "Especially since you both treat books so well."

Ike opened the book and Asa moved close so he could read it at the same time.

Chapter 9

The Diary

August 1, 1700 — Hot again. Trees wilting for lack of rain, and now with the brooks so low, the salt water has moved farther and farther upcreek on each incoming tide. The Indians say that will ruin the fishing if it keeps up. But despite such troubles, this come out a most exciting day. Was mending crab traps on my pier, looked up, and over the reeds here come a sailing vessel making up the creek. A sloop-o'-war she was, and as trim a vessel as ever I've seen, and the only one ever come so far up. Creek's a mile wide most of its way, though not terrible deep outside the channel, but they'd took Wm. Perkins aboard down to King's Point, to show them the channel, and with a following wind they made good time. Still, there never was a better piloting job. In places that channel's not much wider than the ship's hull. Must've dragged her keel now and again, I'd guess, 'cause she rode low in the water like her holds was chock full of something heavy, but she never stopped.

Come in close where the channel lies hard by my pier and give me a good look. A rough looking crew, buccaneers from the look of them, and the Captain had the look of a man you wouldn't want to get caught crosswise of. Stern, he was, with a big jaw that jutted out, and he stood so straight you'd think he had an iron spine. She flew no flags and carried no name on her hull. I waved as she come past, and Mr. Perkins waved back, and then the wind picked up, and she sailed on up to the bend at West Flats, and swept around it right in the middle of the channel. I could see her a long ways 'cause she was so tall, her masts sticking high above the reeds, and I left my work and walked across the ridge to the north side, and watched her sail farther and farther, finally stopping near Boulder Bend where the channel goes dead shallow.

August 2, 1700 — Things got even more interesting today. 'Bout dawn it was, and me just setting out to go crabbing, and upcreek comes a long boat full of red-backed Royal Marines, rowing like the stern of the boat was afire. A blue-clad officer stood in the stern. They rowed right up to me.

"Sir, have you seen a sloop up this way?" the officer asks. Bold and snobbish he was like all them British, and it set my teeth on edge to hear him talk. I nodded.

"When?"

"Mid-morning, yesterday," says I.

"How far up can a ship that size go?"

"Five, six miles. Channel gives out then."

"How many men did she have on board?"

"Couldn't say. Ten, if they was all on deck."

"Can you describe the Captain?"

I told him what I'd seen and he took to rubbing his chin and glancing nervous-like upcreek. "That's him all right," says he.

"That's who?" says I.

"Captain Kidd. We've been chasing him for nearly a fortnight. We came within an eye lash of catching him once, but he's an elusive devil. A pirate he may be, but there's none better at handling a ship."

"What's a famous pirate doing up here?" says I. "Not much of interest but fish, clams, and crabs."

"We've not a clue on that, Sir, but one thing seems certain. We've got him this time. He's trapped as if he had sailed into a bottle and we were the cork." Even as he said it, I could see he wasn't eager to tangle with the famous pirate and truth be knowed, only a mad man would've thought otherwise.

I thought his long boat full of marines made a poor match for the buccaneers I'd seen on Kidd's deck.

"It will pay you to keep your eye peeled," says the officer. "One never knows how a man like Kidd will behave. He could take it in mind to swoop down and burn you out."

I nodded, though I couldn't think why a famous pirate would go rushing about burning down the houses of poor fishermen. But one thing I learnt long ago was never to argue with the King's Navy. It's right full of bullies and braggarts, think the lowest thing next to a snake is a Colonial.

Still, though I'd nothing against Captain William Kidd, nor any reason to think the officer might be right, I resolved to keep watch on the chance that he might be right, and a man can't be too cautious when a famous pirate is nearby. Soon's that boat full of marines had shoved off, I fetched my telescope and clumb up the great white oak at the top of the ridge where I built a platform years ago to watch for hostile Indians. Never did need it. Made friends with the local Indians that summered up to The High Ground by showing them my special crab traps. Then they mostly all died in the smallpox that took off two of my own children.

August 3, 1700 — Hard to write 1700 after all the years of writing 16 first. Makes me feel old to turn up in a new century. But barring sickness I'll last a while yet, Martha too. Got Ezra and Ernest living close by. From the Lookout Tree I saw that the long boat was missing as was Capt. Kidd. But the crew stayed busy, working all though the day on the ship, mending sails and the like. Almost at dark the long boat came back with Capt. Kidd and two other men. Ezra'd tended the traps and we caught crabs in the amount of five bushel. Best set of the summer and a good indication of the season ahead.

August 4, 1700 — Decided to row up the creek, see if I couldn't sell those crabs to Capt. Kidd. Risky business, but I carried no arms, and they'd no reason to think I'd took to spying on them, for they'd not know about the marines having come upcreek. Wouldn't be likely they'd turn on someone who'd done 'em a good turn, and I had something else on my mind too. They bought my crabs for a fair price, I'd provide them with some information they'd need.

Capt. Kidd has a terrible enough reputation, but I found him likable enough, though older than I'd thought. I'd guess his age at close to fifty. He bought all my crabs and never quibbled a bit about the price.

"Captain," says I. "After you passed my pier two days ago, a long boat full of Royal Marines come upcreek. Way they talked, I'd say they're from a man-of-war and their plan is to wait at King's Point till you come out. Said you're in a bottle and they're the cork."

Kidd laughed at that one, all right, and it was a merry sort of sound he made, as if he didn't care one wit for the British. He clapped me on the shoulder. "Mr. Thompson," says he, "you're a valuable man. Provide the best crabs I ever saw, even down in Baltimore. Tomorrow you might just bring up whatever fish you've got and we'll buy the whole boatload. I also have a need for red meat and pork, casked and salted if you can supply that."

I nodded. "Got plenty of venison and pig all right."

"Good. We're low on provisions. Need flour too."

"I'll have my boys bring up what we've got on hand. Wouldn't dare to buy much in King's Point just now. Start a lot of tongues waggin'."

Then his eyes narrowed down some and he rubbed at his big jaw, gently the way people do when they're thinking. "What I wonder, is what you see in this for yourself."

I came right to it. "Pig iron," I says.

He smiled. "What makes you think I don't want that iron. It's worth a lot of money just now."

"Not if it weighs down your sloop so one of them clumsy old man-o'-wars can overhaul her even in a light wind."

"Mr. Thompson, I've carried that iron from the west coast of Africa all the way across the Atlantic. Best quality iron I ever saw. I'm sad to see it go, but you're quite right. With His Majesty's sharks running up my wake, I've no choice but to abandon it. Costly information, but still a good deal more valuable to me than all the iron in the world just now, so it's yours and welcome to it."

"Split was what I had in mind. Wouldn't want it said I tried to take advantage of a man in a tight spot. And I'm prepared to make you another offer," says I. "I don't see your pilot, so I'd guess he went back by Shank's Mare. I'll pilot you out, and have my son waiting at sea by Jacob's Island. We'll want a strong north wind and we'll sail by night. My boys tell me the British are tied up to the main pier, bow out, ready to make sail and fly, and lying up to the pier that way they can rake you with a broadside when you come out. Cannons are all laid to take out your rigging, so I'd guess they were loaded with chain. Now that'd work right smart if you was to sail close in where the channel lies. But there's another channel across the creek behind Finger Island. Not very deep, pretty narrow, but out of range for chain. Your ship, empty, can make it past on the high tide. We'll want to hit just after the tide starts out and then we'll have the wind and the current and we'll go past so quick they won't even get untied from the pier by the time we get to Jacob's Island."

"All this for splitting a load of pig iron? How do I know you're not setting a trap?"

"You're in one now," says I, "and the longer you wait, the worse it'll get. There's a garrison down at Bingham and they'll likely be on the road by now. Take 'em two days at a fast march. Got close to three hundred men down there."

Kidd's eyes narrowed again. "And what would the Governor pay for my capture?"

"Hanged if I know. Don't much care," says I. "Got no use for them lobsterbacks. All they do is lay on more and more taxes."

"I'll send a man to get you in a skiff when we're going

out," Kidd says. "I got saltpeter and silk still aboard. You got a barn for storing, I'll make an arrangement and cut you in for a share of that too once I get things straightened out in Boston. Lord Bellomot's one of my benefactors and I expect I'll be back by fall."

"Bring it down in the dark," I says. "There's a cave, dry as a bone, temperature never varies by more than a couple of degrees. We'll put everything there. Me and my boys will lend a hand. I'll show you where it is. You can pick up your stores at the same time."

"One thing makes me curious, Mr. Thompson. Your dislike of the British seems a good deal stronger than most men I've met."

"No secret there. I had a stand of the best pine a man ever saw and they come and marked it with the King's stamp and cut it off and never paid me so much as a penny. Said it belonged to the King. I'd planned to cut that pine and sell it to shipyards for masts. Then they come back and marked up all the oak. Wasn't a thing for me, but to stand and watch them cut off trees that belonged to me. The land's mine, got a deed for it, but it seems the trees belong to the King. I figure anyone on the wrong side of the British is cleaving to the side I'd choose myself. And mark my words, one day they'll go too far and then the Colonials will rise up. We'll be no easy mark, either."

Kidd smiled at that, all right, a kind of a wolfish smile, and for the first time I understood why few could stand up to him. He had a taste for a scrap all right. "That's why I turned to privateering," says he.

August 5, 1700 — Just past dark they come down in long

boats and worked the night straight through. We carried all the goods back to the cave by horse and wagon and had it done well before light. Captain Kidd stayed in the cave the whole time making sure the goods got proper stowed.

Later that day, from the Lookout Tree, I saw Kidd row off alone in the skiff. It rode low in the water and I could see he had a shovel aboard, and I would guess he had gone off to bury something valuable. Couldn't see just where he went because of the reeds. All I could see was that he went upcreek toward Indian Hill.

August 6, 1700 — Weather change coming, clouds been building up in the west all day. The wind should swing round to the northwest once the storms blow through and then will come his best chance to get out.

Weather broke perfectly, and now the wind is coming north-northwest, and the tide'll pass the high ebb and turn outgoing just after midnight. No moon. I expect to see a boat by ten or eleven, so I'll turn in and get some sleep. I sent Ernest and Ezra off to set up a fish camp at Jacob's Island.

August 7, 1700 — Ten at night, black as pitch when the long boat tied up to the dock and I walked down and climbed aboard. By eleven we hoisted sail and started down, the sloop riding high in the water now, and on the high tide, and with a following wind I never had a faster sail downcreek, though the speed forced me to be especially vigilant in matters of staying to deep water as changes in course had to be calculated a long ways ahead.

The channel on the west side of Finger Island cuts out well above the village and we lowered sail, but for a reefed main, and with the trees on the island to screen our masts and with the dark not a soul stirred. It's pretty much a straight run through the channel and only once did we scrape the keel. Five hundred yards before the end of the island we hoisted full sail and the sloop almost leaped out of the water, for the wind had freshened, and we came busting out into the main creek, and with all that sail on, the lookout spotted us and rang the alarm bell, but by the time they had got anyone up on deck we were out to sea and cutting a straight course through smooth water, due west out of sight of the village to Jacob's Island. We hove too in the lee and the boys come alongside.

"Mr. Thompson," Captain Kidd says with a sly little smile, "you should have been a pirate."

I smiled and shook his hand. "Your goods are safe," says I, "but it might be best to take them out overland. Won't attract near the attention."

He handed me a slip of paper. "This paper gives you the rights to the cargo should something to happen to me," Kidd says. "I only ask that you include my family down in New Amsterdam in the profits from the sale."

"Done," says I and then we shook hands again. "You've got my hand on it."

"And that, I think, Mr. Thompson, is one of the better contracts I've ever made, though I think you ought to have warned me about the cave spirits," he says.

Now there he had the better of me and I thought perhaps he'd got into the grog. "Spirits?" I asked.

"Aye, spirits," he says, "spirits if ever there were."

"I'd known, I'd've warned you," says I.

Then Kidd smiled. "Might be my imagination," he says.

"Never cared much for caves."

With that I climbed over the side and dropped into the boat with Ezra and Ernest and we put back into the island. It would arouse no suspicion. We camped there regularly when we were fishing. From the top of the island we watched him sail off toward Boston. About an hour later the man-o'-war hove into view and slowly sailed past. Clumsy, big ship it was that couldn't even sail well in a following sea, but kept driving her bow down into every swell.

August 8, 1700 — Had a visit from the Colonial Administrator, Sir Robert Molton. Wanted to know how Kidd had made his getaway.

I'd never seen Sir Robert, but at a distance before, and for a second or two his haughty manner and fancy dress, made me forget just how far away we were from England. But I recovered before I started to talk. "Well, you got me there," says I. "Never knew he'd gone, till he had."

"Mr. Thompson," says he, puffing himself up like a great toad, "how is it he knew about the channel behind Finger Island?"

"Now how would I know anything about that? A tricky devil like Kidd, he most likely knew about that before he ever came up into the creek. Not a man to sail into a trap, wouldn't you say?"

Well, I had him there all right and he left off the questions and went back downcreek with the soldiers from the local garrison doing the rowing.

Asa looked across at Ike, and neither of them could think what to say. It was true. Kidd had been here and he had buried something here. But where was the cave? How, in all their wandering around had they never found it? A cave that big was pretty hard to miss.

"Is that exciting enough?" Miss Jameson asked as she came up behind them and laid a copy of a map on the table.

"Wow ..." Ike said. "Kidd was really here."

Miss Jameson smiled. "If Josiah Thompson is to be believed."

"Is there any reason not to believe him?" Asa asked.

"Well, there were always stories about the family. And they were by any measure, eccentric, but I can't see why Josiah would have made that up. In the boxes I also came across this map. It's the oldest I've ever seen of the creek and Josiah made it, I'd guess for his own use. Without it I don't think the places he mentions make much sense.

"There's more, but it's not as exciting," Miss Jameson said. "Captain Kidd was hanged in May of 1701 in England and Josiah Thompson sold the goods in Boston and gave half the money to Mrs. Kidd. Then he went looking for the treasure. He spent the rest of his life looking for it, but he never found it. You're going to look, you ought to read all that, because it tells where he looked."

She smoothed her dress again, across her flat stomach, a habit that had been known to irritate some of the larger women in town, who resented Miss Jameson's slender form. "It's sad reading," she said. "So many wasted years, though I suppose there's a lesson to be learned about getting obsessed by something to the point where it consumes you."

If they heard her warning, they showed no sign and as soon as she left they went back to reading, noting all the places Josiah Thompson had looked. Hour by hour the list grew and grew, and when they had turned the last page they felt as if they would never find the treasure, for it seemed as though he must have looked everywhere. But at least they had his map and with that they could coordinate the places he had looked, with the creek as they knew it.

While Asa puzzled over the notes, Ike pulled the encyclopedia for A and looked up albino. It didn't tell him much beyond what he knew, but at least it confirmed what he had guessed. Albinos have weak vision, especially in the light. That would give them an edge if they went back to The High Ground, and now, knowing that Kidd had buried something up there somewhere, they had no choice but to go back. And yet, he was pretty sure nothing had been buried there. The tip-off was the big tree stump that Whitey had been so excited about. Asa had to be right about that. It had been a great tall tree then and Kidd had used it as a landmark, not worrying about whether the tree would still be there because he planned to be back in under a year.

But still it was important to remember that they were talking about Captain William Kidd and he was nothing if not sly.

They walked slowly toward the wharf and suddenly Ike poked him in the ribs and smiled. "Hey, look who's coming down the street."

Asa blushed as he looked at Ashley Weathers.

"Hi," she said as she stopped in front of them. "I didn't think you ever came into town."

"Had to sell our clams," Asa said.

"Are you going to the festival?"

She was so pretty he found it hard to think. "What festival. There's gonna be a festival?"

"Labor Day Weekend. It's called Captain Kidd Days."

"I never heard anything about it, did you, Ike?"

Ike shook his head.

"They're gonna announce it this week. There'll be a big picnic, and games, and dancing, and even fireworks."

"Sounds cool," Asa said. "I'll be there."

"Everybody's going," Ashley said as she looked directly into his eyes. "I had a great time at the dance, Asa."

"Me too," he said.

"Well, I gotta meet my Mom," she said. "Call me, okay."

"Okay, I'll call," Asa said.

They watched her walk away and then turned toward the wharf and Ike made sure they were well out of range before he spoke. "Looks like true love to me," he said.

Asa just grinned.

Chapter 10

The Puzzle

Fighting upcreek against the tide nearly doubled the time it took to get home, though neither Ike nor Asa much noticed the time till they stormed into Meg Clark's kitchen nearly overcome with hunger. Meg stood with her arms folded, angry over their having broken a long-standing rule about reporting in when you had run late.

"You're just lucky you've got such a good friend in Miss Jameson," Meg said. "She thought you might be late, and for some reason thought you might not call, so she called to let me know you'd left the library."

Asa said nothing and Ike kept well in the background. A mother's rampage was a lot like a line squall. The best way to survive was to put your bow into the swells and maintain just enough way to steer, while you rode it out.

"Now I suppose," Meg said, "that you're probably hungry and you've come charging into my kitchen right over my clean floor looking for something to eat?"

"We are kinda hungry, Mom," Asa said. "I'm sorry I didn't call. I never looked at my watch and then we caught the outgoing tide coming upcreek."

Despite her anger over their getting back nearly three hours late, Meg fixed them fish salad sandwiches, though not without delivering an impromptu lecture about the dangers of the water and how the people on shore worried. They had heard it all a hundred times before, but still they listened, perhaps because of the times they had waited for their fathers to return in weather so bad they couldn't punch a radio call through. Not a year went by that some fisherman along the coast didn't go down. They knew they should have called, and there could be no argument, no excuse. If you were old enough to run your own boat, then you were old enough to follow the rules. The rules were absolute. That's what saved your life and kept those who waited on shore from worrying.

Somewhat abashed, they carried their lunch to the picnic table in the front yard, surrounded by its white picket fence, and then spread out the brand new chart they had bought in King's Point, and weighted it at each corner with a rock to keep the breeze from folding it over.

They used a compass to orient the chart by putting the top to the north, which made it not only easier to read, but easier to understand as they sat facing north, looking upcreek. Then, as they ate, they compared the chart with Josiah's map. They drew in the old creek bed and marked the old names of places on the creek on the new chart.

"Do you see Indian Hill anywhere?" Asa asked.

"I think that's what we call The High Ground."

"How about Little Fishhook?"

Ike stabbed his finger down onto the map. "It's one of the fingernails now."

"He says he searched from The Fishhook to Westering Run."

"Westering Run must be this fingernail here to the southwest of Boulder Bend," Ike said.

"But how can that be?"

"It's where the creek bit itself off," Ike said. "And it's the only place where the creek ever ran due west."

Asa stared down at the chart. "What do you make of this mark?" He pointed to a circle that had been inked in.

Ike looked closely at the map. "I don't know."

"If it's meant to mark something, then whatever it is lies on that hill." Asa pointed off to the northeast to the big, rounded knob of a hill about an eighth of a mile away.

Ike picked up the ruler and measured the distance from the creek to the hill on the chart and then on Josiah's map. "This is a pretty accurate map, Asa. The scale is almost perfect." He set the ruler down and picked up his sandwich.

"Isn't that kind of unusual? I thought old maps weren't usually in scale."

"They weren't." Ike leaned out farther, taking a bite of sandwich and dropping a piece of fish on the chart.

"Hey, Ike! Watch it, will you?"

"Oops. Sorry." With a napkin he wiped up the fish and the spot of mayonnaise. "Jeez, Asa, you're crotchety as a settin' hen. Lighten up, will you?"

Asa smiled apologetically. "Sorry," he said. "I'm getting a little over eager, I think."

"I'm thinking, Asa, that this map is accurate enough so

we could measure the distance from the dock he marked here, to the house, and then pace it off from the old pilings and find the cellar hole."

"I'll bet," Asa said, "that the circle marks the cave."

"Then we could pace that off too. Just cut a compass line from the cellar hole to the hill and that should tell us."

Asa smiled. "Sure is handy knowing navigation," he said.

Ike looked off toward the hill sticking well above the trees. "What did you think of that remark in the diary about spirits in the cave?" His eyes had widened considerably. He was always uneasy about ghosts and spirits.

"Maybe Kidd found the old Indian burial ground."

"In the cave?"

"Why not?"

Ike shrugged. "I never heard of the Indians around here using caves to bury their dead, but I never heard of them not doing it either." Ike grinned. "We've got a lot of poking around to do."

"But first we go for the treasure, right?"

"Right." Ike looked out across the lawn to the creek curving off into the bend it made around South Ridge where they sat. His gaze wandered away from the trees which dominated the ridge to the creek, and then to the miles and miles of marshes stretching off to the west and south and north. Nothing but reeds and grasses and water and mud and millions of animals from small to large. His mother knew the name of each bird that lived in the marshes and woods, and she belonged to the Nature Conservancy and a bunch of other conservation groups, and she and Mrs. Clark had written letters to their senators and congressmen and the governor, trying to find a way to protect the marshes. So far they had stopped King's Point from expanding their piers and dredging the marsh to the north of the village for a marina. Now they were trying to get a law made down in Washington to protect the marshes forever. He liked that idea very much, despite the fights he and Asa had gotten into with kids whose parents thought the marshes ought to be dug out or filled in.

He thought about the fingernail ponds and how you never knew they were there until you got up high enough to see them the way they had from The High Ground. "The creek sure followed a different bed back then."

"Sure did." Asa looked up from the chart. "How much water would Kidd have needed to get up to Boulder Bend?"

Ike shrugged. "Probably about fifteen feet, maybe a little more. In the channel there's twenty feet even at low tide all the way to Boulder Bend." He pointed to the depth readings on the chart. "High water there's over twenty-five feet, thirty in places."

"When do we start?"

"Tomorrow?"

"The sooner the better. But we still have to dig quahogs."

"If we get an early start, we can combine the trips. But we've got tomorrow anyway, because the Benbow won't need more until Friday at the earliest."

"But we haven't tried the other restaurants yet. I'll bet Mrs. Sparks at the hotel would take some."

"Maybe we could call them."

"We could try. It's not like they don't know who we are."

But they still had most of the afternoon before them, and tomorrow seemed a long, long way off, and the idea of just calling up the restaurants was a little daunting.

"Say," Ike said. "Do you think we could find the cave?"

"Sure," Asa said. "If we can't find it by compass, I thought of another way. He used a horse and wagon to haul the stuff to the cave, right?"

"Uh-huh."

"So we look for an old, old wagon track somewhere near where his house stood, and that should lead us to the cave."

"Do you think we've got time to do it today?"

"It'll be a lot easier if we can find the foundation."

Both their heads turned toward the water and the flat blat of the horn on *The Shitepoke* as it rounded the bend. "Boy, they finished early," Asa said. "Hey, now you'll get to see Fishbone!" Tar abandoned the shade and rushed down the hill to the pier.

After his encounter with Whitey and his bad dream, Ike thought that about the last person he wanted to meet would be The Fishbone, but neither could he leave.

"Com'on," Asa said, "we'll walk down to the pier."

They stood on the old, weathered planks of the pier watching *The Shitepoke* coming up through the slack water, following the channel closely now with the tide dead low.

"Darn it!" Asa said. "I forgot to look up about mussels this morning. I was gonna get some books on mussels to see what we'd need to do to set up our mussel farm."

"You know what else we ought to do is seed our own quahog beds." Ike raised his arm and pointed at the shore across the creek. "That all used to be great clamming ground."

"Yeah, but then the clam goons in King's Point will find out about it and steal them."

"Maybe we could find a way to rent the ground the way they do for oyster beds down in Long Island Sound."

"We dump part of each haul we make into those beds. Then after we know they've spawned we can take the adults."

The Shitepoke, with Fishbone standing on deck, slipped up to the pier and Asa caught the line and made her fast as Tom put the engine in reverse and pulled the stern in against the pilings. Fishbone jumped ashore with the stern line and tied it off on the big, rounded bollard between the pilings.

"Good catch?" Asa asked.

"The best," Tom said as he stepped off the boat. "How're you doing, Ike? You met Fishbone Watson yet? Fishbone, this is Ike Wilson, lives just up around the bend. His father owns *The Marlinspike*."

"How do'y'do, Ike Wilson," Fishbone said and he stuck out his hand and smiled.

Ike smiled back and shook his hand. "Hello," he said, hoping the anxiety he felt did not show. "What'd you catch?"

"Stripers," Tom said. "I wouldn't have believed it, but Fishbone spent last night catching eels 'cause he'd heard you could catch stripers just south of Jacob's Island, and by golly, we did get into 'em. Took twenty-five big stripers, not a one under forty pounds. When that played out we set for haddock and filled the holds."

They walked up the hill toward the house, Tar keeping to one side instead of leading as he usually did, and he never took his eyes off Fishbone.

"Fishbone," Tom said, "I think this day deserves a beer, whyn't you come up to the house."

"Wouldn't mind a beer a'tall," Fishbone said.

Not until they came through the gate, did the boys remember their charts and the notes still sitting on the table, right next to the walk.

Tom spotted them first. "Now what have we got here?" he said as he stopped and looked down at the table. "Looks like you boys invested in a brand new chart. You marking your new clamming grounds?"

"That's right," Asa said. "We were just getting started when we heard the horn on the boat."

"Better keep it well hidden. Plenty of scalawags down to King's Point'd like to see that, you can bet. News about your quahogs is all over town."

They watched carefully as Fishbone looked down at the chart and then the notes. He said nothing, but they saw from the glint in his eye that he had guessed they were up to a good deal more than marking out their clamming grounds.

The boys waited by the table, and once the men had gone inside they rolled up the chart and the notes and carried them in through the front door and upstairs to Asa's room. They stuffed them between the mattress and the box spring on his bed, and then went down to the kitchen.

"I'm going over to Ike's," Asa said.

"Just be back by five," Meg said. "And be on time, Asa."

"Okay, Mom," he said.

They had crossed the lawn to the edge of the woods on the road to the Wilson's when Ike stopped. "You still want to look for that old foundation?"

"Sure. We got plenty of time, and with any luck we can even find the cave."

"I never heard of a cave around here, did you?"

"No, but it must be hidden somehow. We haven't got time to use the compass, but maybe we could find the cart track. Once we find that I don't see how we can miss."

Chapter 11

Josiah's Cave

They didn't so much find the foundation as nearly fall into it, Ike grabbing Asa's arm just before he took the step which would have sent him tumbling into the hole. They walked around it several times, looking down into the empty foundation with its laid-up stone walls, trying to imagine what Josiah Thompson had looked like and what his house had looked like.

"Look at how big the trees are." Asa pointed to the thick sugar maples which had taken root in the hole. "The Thompsons must have left a long time ago."

"I wonder why they went away," Ike said.

Asa shrugged. "Maybe the diary says."

"After we find the gold I'm going to read the rest of it. I'd like to know."

And while Asa admitted to some curiosity along those very lines, just now he had the cave on his mind, and Asa seldom allowed his imagination to push him off course. He pointed to a faint path in the woods.

"That must have been the road up from the pier. Probably they had the land pretty well cleared so we won't be able to tell much by where the trees grow. We'll have to look for a place where the ground is worn into ruts." He pointed off to his left. "You circle that way and I'll go the other way. If we don't find anything we'll keep circling farther and farther from the cellar hole."

Ike nodded and set off, walking as Asa did, very, very slowly with his eyes to the ground, pushing aside the brush with his feet. Now and then he stopped and looked off toward the creek, trying to imagine what it must have looked like to Josiah Thompson when he had stood there watching Captain Kidd's ship making upcreek on the tide. In his mind he could see the sails billowing in the following wind from the sea, pennants flying, and a man with a sounding lead in the bow and another man in the crow's nest aloft. Then he drifted back to reality and began poking along, looking for wagon ruts, knowing they were there somewhere, and it was only a matter of time before they found them.

The first and second circles turned up nothing, but the third time they made the loop, Ike found the track. "Asa, over here! I think this is it."

Asa ran to where Ike stood, dropped down on his knees, and felt the ground. "Yeah, this is it, all right," he said as he cleared away the dried leaves." He stood up and they started walking, stopping frequently to make sure they had not strayed from the track. The trees here cut off the breeze from the marshes, and the heat made them sweat. Then the mosquitoes closed in. Both boys pulled out their bug spray, spreading it on their arms below their tee shirts, and on their necks and faces, and even their ankles below the bottoms of their jeans.

"At least the black flies are gone now," Asa said. "I can live with the mosquitoes."

"I don't like anything that bites."

Up ahead the brush thinned out and they walked among taller, much older trees, and there they had little difficulty following the track. Only where it crossed the road that ran down to Ike's house did they lose it, but by walking out in overlapping semicircles they found it again soon enough; a straight line now, running right back toward the high knoll which rose in a great dome above the ledges.

The track ended at the bottom of a low cliff in a great pile of small rocks which over the years the frost had cracked away from the naked rock face that angled back into the hillside. They stood looking up at the jumble of rock at the base of the cliff.

"Funny looking kinda rock," Asa said. "Most of the rock around here is granite, but I don't think this is."

Ike looked skeptically at the jumbled rock in the talus slope. "Sure is a lot of it."

"Sure is," Asa said.

"Do you think it's behind the fallen rocks?" Ike asked.

"Must be."

"No way to find out but dig, I guess."

"Might as well start," Asa said.

The rocks, basketball sized, for the most part took no great effort to move, and they started at the top and rolled them to the sides, letting them bounce down and crash off into the woods. Here at least the breeze blew steadily and though the work made them sweat, the moisture, evaporating quickly in the dry air, helped keep them cool.

"You're right about Fishbone," Ike said. "He's easily as scary as Whitey." He grabbed onto an angular piece of rock, heaved it upward, pushed it to the side, and watched it topple down the slope. "I'd sure like to know what they're thinking."

"You mean whether we have anything to worry about?"

"Yeah. Suppose they think we have a better map, or that we might get our fathers into it. We could all be in serious trouble, Asa."

Asa grappled onto a large rock, straining with his legs, managing to roll it high enough so it fell over the lip to the ground below. "I wonder if Fishbone knows Whitey is up there. I'll bet he doesn't. I don't think he had enough time to go that far upcreek. He knows he's around somewhere, but maybe if we can find a way to tip him off, he'll keep away from us, and he'll keep Whitey busy at the same time."

"Sure, and then they find the treasure instead of us!"

"I wonder if they have the real map or maybe a fake," Asa said as he stopped to wipe the sweat from his face. "Whitey's dug an awful lot of holes."

"But now he's found that old stump."

"I'd like to have another look around up there, and we need to dig more clams too."

"Who cares about clams! Do you know what we could buy with Kidd's treasure?"

"Com'on, Ike, do you really believe we'll find the treasure? I mean, sure, it'll be great fun looking for it, but think of all the people who tried, and not even Josiah Thompson found it, and he probably knew more about it than anybody.

At least with the clams we know what we've got. We know where to get them and we've got a good solid market."

"You mean you'd really consider taking time away from looking for the treasure?"

"I thought you didn't want to go back up to The High Ground."

"No, I got it figured. We can handle Whitey. He's an albino, and I read in the library how albinos don't see very well in daylight. We can easily sneak in and find out what he's doing."

"You still planning to take your rifle?"

"I am."

"Okay, tomorrow we go. But ... we're also going to dig clams, okay? We have to have something to tell our folks, remember."

An hour later they were still pulling rocks, though now they had tired and each rock seemed heavier than the one before. They had scraped and scuffed their hands on the sharp edges of the rocks, and when they stood up and looked at how much they had done, the job seemed hopeless, for as they dug deeper, the pile grew wider, and they had to move a great many more stones.

"This is harder work than I thought," Ike said.

"Sure is." Asa wiped the sweat from his forehead.

Neither of them was eager to go back to work.

"If we quit now we'd have plenty of time to get home for supper," Ike said.

Asa looked at his watch. "We've still got lots of time. How about we do ten more rocks each."

"Okay. But that's all. My hands hurt."

"Just ten," Asa said, "just ten good size rocks apiece and

then we'll quit."

They bent over and began again, and then suddenly, at five rocks each, an opening appeared, and the cool air from the cave came rushing out at them, dry and attic old and smelling of places they had been told over and over not to go.

"Look! That's it!" Asa shouted. Now, energized by success, they worked at full speed till rock by rock and stone by stone, they had made an opening big enough to crawl through. Then the warnings about climbing into caves stopped them and they sat looking down into the black hole, pulled back by the warnings and energized by the pull of the unknown.

"We need a light," Asa said.

"And we need to move more rocks too."

"Caves are dangerous," Asa said.

"But we have to find out whether maybe Josiah left something here that can help us."

"Maybe he did, but I don't think so."

"Suppose he was trickier than we think? Suppose he found the gold and never told anybody?"

"Why would he do that? And if he had would he have written what he did in his diary?"

"Maybe somebody would have claimed it and taken it away from him," Ike said. "After all, it was stolen, you know. So maybe he hid it here and blew up the cliff so nobody would find the cave." Ike bent forward and looked into the opening. "The only way to find out is go in and look around."

"We'll need a light, and the one thing we have to be sure of is that it's safe."

"If we move just a few more rocks maybe it'll let in

enough light so we can see. We'll only go in a few feet, or until the light from the opening gives out."

Asa shook his head. He wanted nothing more than to go into the cave, but he already felt guilty enough about going upcreek beyond Boulder Bend. Still, what could happen? They had cleared away plenty of rocks, and he saw no danger of a cave in. "Okay, but only until the light gives out."

"All right!" Ike shouted, and they began moving more and more rocks until they had opened a hole nearly six feet in all directions, taking particular care, at Asa's insistence, to taper the lower lip of the opening outward so that in the event of a cave-in most of the rubble would roll clear of the opening instead of catching on the lip and closing the hole they'd made.

"Who's first?" Asa asked.

"Me," Ike said and he slipped though the hole and lowered himself down, facing forward and planting his backside firmly before moving farther down. Asa followed.

Over time dust had fallen to the floor of the cave, and the fine powder puffed outward from beneath their feet as they stepped gingerly toward the gloom ahead. It surprised them to see how far back into the cave the light traveled, and as they walked, and the light grew steadily more pale and dim, their eyes adjusted. The walls of the cave rose straight up to over six feet before curving in a smooth arc to the ceiling. They walked slowly, alert to the slightest sound, tense and ready to run for the opening.

"Did you notice how good the air is?" Asa asked. "There must be another opening somewhere."

"Another entrance?"

"Maybe."

"What time is it?" Ike asked.

Asa lifted his arm and held it up into the dim light from the mouth of the cave. "Four-thirty. We probably should head back."

"Let's go a little farther. Look, there's a wall there. Let's go to that."

They walked forward, to the wall, stopped, and looked back to the mouth of the cave.

"How far do you think it is to the opening?" Asa asked. He looked back the way they had come, and now the hole seemed no larger than what a rat would choose. "Sixty, maybe seventy yards?"

"Doesn't seem like much of a cave. When we were reading the diary, I got the idea that it was much bigger."

"So did I. You could hardly fit all the stuff they took from Kidd's ship in here."

They walked left along the wall to where it joined the side wall of the cave, and then retraced their steps, and suddenly they came to an opening they had not seen in the dim light. Beyond, the blackness hung thick and dense and they could not see into it.

"We'll have to come back with a light," Ike said. "I can't see anything."

The noise at the mouth of the cave started as a low rumble and then a roar as rocks from above came tumbling down in a waterfall rush, the sound louder and louder, and then finally tapering off to dead quiet, and when it stopped the light had gone, and they stood in blackness, absolute blackness which not even the blackest night they had ever seen could match.

"Don't move," Asa said quickly. "Don't move until we

find out if we can see anything. I read once that if you wander around in the dark you lose any sense of where you are."

"We're trapped ..." Ike said, and his voice sounded small and faint. "How will anyone find us? Nobody but us knows about the cave."

Asa reached out in the dark and put his hand on Ike's arm. "Take it easy," he said. "We've got plenty of air and in a minute or two we'll know whether there's any light."

"How can you be so calm?" Ike asked, knowing even as he asked the question that he had never seen Asa panic over anything. The worse the trouble got, the steadier Asa got. They were a good match. Asa took care of the panic and he took care of the imagination. But right now they were pulling in opposite directions.

"Take hold of my shirt," Asa said and when he felt Ike grab on, he put his hands against the end wall and walked along, always keeping one hand against the cold rock. It seemed to take forever before he found the corner where it met the side wall of the cave, and then he moved along that wall until he stumbled over the loose rock that had fallen in and closed the cave. "Go slowly, Ike. We're going to climb up the rocks to the top of the cave. Then we can start pulling them down. Only pull away rocks that are warm when you touch them. Those are the rocks that came in where we opened the entrance. The others will be cold."

How did he do that? Ike asked himself. How did he stay so calm, how did he think of something like the rocks being warm? Why wasn't he scared? How could you not be scared? What if they couldn't get out? Maybe all anyone would ever find would be their skeletons ... nothing but the bones of two boys who hadn't listened to their parents. Their ghosts would haunt the cave forever. "Do you think we're gonna get out?"

"We'll get out," Asa said.

"Do you think somebody caused the landslide?" Ike asked.

"Naw, we just weren't careful enough when we dug our way in. We must have loosened some rock above." But he did not believe that, because he remembered having checked carefully to make sure they had not built their own trap. The only question was who had started the slide, and while only Fishbone was around, he did not discount Whitey having walked down from The High Ground. With a crazy man like that, anything was possible.

"There must be a lot of rock," Ike said. "I can't see any light at all. How long do you think it will take us."

"I don't know, but if we're lucky we'll only be late for supper."

"I don't feature spending the night in here, Asa."

"Me neither," Asa said. "But it could be worse. Suppose we'd been standing here when the rocks came down." As they climbed higher he swept the air above his head, feeling for the ceiling of the cave.

"What if it caves in again?"

"We'll have to be careful when we pull the rocks away. I just hope they aren't too big." Suddenly his hand above his head touched the ceiling. "We're at the top," he said. "You stay here. I'll try to find the warm rocks." He kept one hand on the ceiling of the cave to make sure he did not drift downward, and in the dark it seemed as if he had traveled a long way before the rocks beneath his hands still held the warmth they had gathered from the summer sun.

"Ike, feel for the ceiling of the cave. Keep a hand on it and move toward me. And be ready to roll clear if things start to move."

"Okay," Ike said. He felt the panic rise quickly as he placed his hand against the cold rock at the top of the cave, but he moved along as fast as he could over the broken and jagged rocks, forcing himself to concentrate on the task at hand instead of their situation. He tried to see the funny side of what had happened, but he found little to laugh at. What was funny about being sealed in a pitch black cave? Nothing. There was nothing funny about this at all. And nobody knew where they were and ... and then suddenly the rocks felt warm. "Asa?"

"Right here. Let's start digging."

The rocks seemed to come away easily at first, and each time he pulled a rock loose, Asa waited, listening for the sound of another cave in. But the only sounds came from the rocks they pulled free as they rumbled and clattered down the pile to the floor of the cave. "Ike, save your strength. I have no idea how long this is gonna take."

How, Ike wondered, could he stay so calm? There was not the least sign of panic in his voice. He was certain they'd get out, and all they had to do was keep working, pulling away the stones, and suddenly there would be a hole, and they could climb on out into the daylight. Why did he doubt that? What made him think that might not happen?

They worked steadily, rock by rock, and though their muscles were worn and tired from having dug their way in, the need to get back out gave them added energy.

Asa reached up into the dark and discovered he could now reach around the mouth of the cave to the outside wall.

"Wait a minute, Ike. Can you reach the outside wall yet?"

"Yup."

"Me too. There must be a lot of rock above. Keep working, but be ready to dive back out of the way, because some of that rock is probably going to come through the hole we're making."

"Okay."

They worked more carefully now, prying the rocks loose, their hands sore from the abrasive surface of the stone. With each stone they anticipated another cave in, and each time it didn't happen they sighed with relief and grabbed onto another stone. And then Ike pulled away what seemed to be a stone no bigger than a football and with a rush the rock above came pouring through and both boys whirled away from the opening. Had they not been ready they would have been swept to the floor of the cave and buried in the rubble which came crashing into the cave with a roar like a passing train. But with the rubble came the light and they scrambled through the hole and out into the day, coughing and choking from the dust.

For several minutes they sat atop the rocks in the blinding light. Then Asa stood and looked up the slope above the cave. He could see no loose rock above the cave entrance now. He looked at his watch. "We're late for supper," he said.

"We better tell the truth this time," Ike said.

"No. Not yet. I want to look into the back of that cave and if we tell our folks what happened, we'll never get the chance."

"Maybe we can get our dads to help us make the entrance safe," Ike said.

"They won't take the time, Ike. They can't. Not at this

time of year with the fishing good."

Ike nodded and wiped his eyes with the backs of his hands. "How about we tell them we were looking for Josiah's cave and we lost track of time."

"That sounds okay."

"Let's go. The sooner we get home, the better that's going to sound."

They stood up to climb down from the rocks and Ike stopped and looked off to the north. "You can see The High Ground from here," he said. "If the leaves were off the trees, you could even see Whitey's camp." He rubbed his eyes again. "With a telescope I'll bet we could see him digging."

"It'd be safer than going up there," Asa said.

At the bottom of the pile the boys stopped to dust off.

"Ike, maybe we shouldn't even mention the cave."

"You're right," Ike said. "One look at us and they'd guess we'd already found it."

"We'll say we were building a fort. How's that sound?"

"To me, it sounds fine, but I don't know whether my mother will bite. We haven't built any forts in a long time."

"We'll say we got a plan from the library about how to build a stone fort."

"I don't like telling all these lies, Asa."

"Me neither. It always makes things worse in the end." He looked up. "Do this. Don't say a word unless you're pressed into it."

"Okay."

They walked off toward their homes, and as soon as they had gotten out of sight of each other, they took off at a run.

Chapter 12

The Burglar

Asa stood on the pier and watched his father and Fishbone head downcreek in his boat to go eeling. He waited until they disappeared into the gathering dark, waited until he heard the motor suddenly fade as they rounded the bend out of sight. Then he stepped into the boathouse and snapped on the light so if his mother should happen to look down toward the pier she would think he was working.

With Tar at his side he crossed the lawn to the cabin, keeping low so his silhouette would not show against the silvery water of the creek. He slipped up onto the porch, staying away from the windows and the light from inside. "Tar," he said, "sit. Stay."

The dog obeyed instantly, sitting with his head cocked, his ears up, alert to every sound.

For awhile he watched the house, waiting until he could see his mother moving past the upstairs windows as she settled Missy for the night. Then he drew back the screen door, opening it only wide enough to squeeze past so he did not allow the rusty spring its customary squeal.

In the quiet he could hear his heart racing, and he drew a deep breath, trying to calm himself enough to think clearly. Where to look first? He crossed to the bureau, surprised to find that Fishbone had not used it. He kept his clothes stored in his seabag, which, Asa decided, meant he was ready for a quick departure. But would he keep the map in the seabag? It didn't seem likely, but he decided to check it first.

He stood the worn, heavy canvas bag on the chair next to the bed, carefully untied the drawstring at the top, and pulled the bag open. All the clothes were rolled in proper fashion, and he removed each item, unrolled it on the bed, then rolled it back up, matching, as closely as he could, the way he had found it. He kept things in order as he worked down through the bag so he could put them back in the same order, and perhaps not leave Fishbone suspecting someone had gone through his stuff.

It was slow work, and it looked to him as if some of the stuff had been in the bag a long time, but near the bottom he found a heavy package wrapped in a plastic bag. He opened it slowly and pulled out the oily cloth, and when he unwrapped that he found a Colt revolver. He stood looking at the gun for several minutes, trying to decide whether to take it or leave it there. Certainly it made sense to disarm Fishbone if he could, but there was no question he would miss the gun. He opened the cylinder and took out the cartridges, dropped them into his pocket, closed the gun, wiped it carefully, and put it back the way he had found it. Maybe he wouldn't check to see whether it was loaded. And while that seemed unlikely in anyone used to handling guns, it was the best plan he could come up with.

What struck him as odd was that in looking through the rest of the bag he found no other cartridges. Did he really only have six? Where else would he keep them? If you owned a gun, you had to have more than six cartridges. Heck, they had boxes and boxes of ammo at the house, at least two boxes for each gun, including the revolvers and the automatic. He began putting the gear back into the seabag, carefully duplicating the way he had found things.

That done he stood and looked around. Where else? The bathroom? Maybe he had a shaving kit with a pocket in it. But he found only a razor and a toothbrush, some shaving soap and toothpaste. No kit. Did he keep the map with him? If he did then it would be wrapped in plastic and sealed to keep it from being ruined if he fell overboard, or even from the sodden nets when they finished a trawl and dropped the flopping mass of fish onto the deck to be sorted.

He stepped back into the main room and stopped to listen for the sound of the outboard but the night offered only the rasping katydids and crickets, and then he froze and crouched down as he heard Tar growl. He backed into the corner made by the main wall and the bathroom wall, and drew the door back to conceal himself from anyone looking through the windows. Tar growled again and then he broke, his bark big and deep as he trotted toward the woods. He heard the big dog snort to clear his nose and test the air, and then he growled again, a deep, menacing sound, and suddenly he heard something run off through the woods. A deer? No, the sound was wrong for a deer. Whatever it was, it ran on two feet, and he slipped into the darkened bathroom and closed the door, and through the window he saw a flash of white fading rapidly into the dark. Whitey! And probably it had been Whitey at the cave too. From now on he'd keep Tar with him. Good old Tar ... the best dog ever.

He waited until he heard the dog settle back down, and then he stepped out into the main room and looked around, trying to make himself see what he had not seen so far. He marked off each item in his mind; plates, pots and pans, dish soap, sponge, a cup of pencils, Scotch tape, empty beer bottles, trash can ... wait! He couldn't remember seeing the tape here before. Why would he need tape? Maybe the map had been torn and he taped it together. Or maybe ... just maybe he had used the tape to hide the map where you would not expect anyone to look. He scanned the room again. Under the counter tops. He opened each door and looked at the undersides of the counters. Nothing. He sat at the table in the center of the room and looked around. Under the bed? He got down on his hands and knees and lay on his back and looked at the springs. Nothing. He slid back out and sat up and there was the table looking right at him. He slipped under it, so certain the map would be there that he was shocked when he didn't find it.

Disappointed, he simply lay on the floor staring up at the dark wood. If it wasn't here, then where could he have hidden it? In the dark below the table his eyes adjusted slowly to the light and then he noticed the drawer, and as a last resort he reached up and pushed the drawer open, and there it was, folded and taped neatly in place. He pulled it free, using great care not to tear the paper, and then he sat at the table, opened the map, pulled a sheet of tracing paper from his shirt pocket, and laid it over the old yellowed paper.

He worked quickly, starting at the top, including each detail, every mark, even if it seemed as if the mark meant nothing. And suddenly his head came up. The outboard! Too soon! Why were they coming back so soon? He concentrated on the tracing, working as fast as he could, hoping he would have time enough to finish it. Tar had heard the boat, and he heard him growl and head down toward the pier. He was sweating, and he wiped his forehead to make sure no drops fell onto the paper as he struggled to complete the map, working very fast, and still making sure he missed nothing. He could hear the high snarl of the engine as the boat drew closer. Almost done. And then finally he drew in the last lines, folded the map , climbed under the table, and taped it in place.

The boat was very close now, and he slipped quickly out of the cabin by the back door, keeping to the woods, staying low as he worked his way down to the boathouse. Once inside he picked up the walking stick he had been working on, clamped it into the vice, picked up the draw shave, and began curling away layers of wood. He worked fast, holding the shave by both handles and pulling it toward him across the surface of the stick, each pull adding to the rapidly growing pile of shavings, and then when he heard them reach the pier, he set the drawshave on the bench, turned on the pier lights, and stepped outside.

"Catch many?" he asked as he stepped onto the pier.

"Got God's own amount of 'em," his father said. "This here Fishbone brings a man the best kind of luck. We'll clean up on stripers tomorrow for sure."

He waited until they had stowed the eels aboard *The Shitepoke*, and then walked to the boathouse with his father and Fishbone to store the eeling gear.

Fishbone glanced at the pile of shavings. "Looks like you been busy."

"I'd have got more done if Tar hadn't got himself all worked up over something. I heard it run off. Probably a moose from the sound."

"Most likely," his father said as they stepped back outside and he switched off the lights. "Be up at four, Fishbone, and we'll make a good dollar."

"See you then," Fishbone said.

He walked quietly up to the house alongside his father, so eager to compare Fishbone's map to the other charts that he had all he could do to keep from bolting ahead. He didn't even dare talk for fear the eagerness in his voice would rouse his father's suspicions.

Chapter 13

Map And Compass

Asa opened the door to the Wilson's boathouse to find Ike hard at work tearing down his outboard. "Figured out what's wrong?" he asked.

"Not yet." Ike straightened up and wiped his hands on a rag he had picked from the work bench. "You get in any trouble last night?"

"It was close, but I think I got by. How about you?"

"Mom made me take a shower before I ate."

"Me too."

Ike went back to work on his engine. "There's weather coming. A nor'easter, Dad says."

"Maybe it won't be too bad."

"That's it, Asa, take the bright side. Take my job. You're supposed to be the gloomy partner in this operation." Ike changed the socket on his wrench. "But I been thinking about this and I think we're in over our heads. These guys are mean,

Asa. Like yesterday at the cave. That slide wasn't any accident. Somebody started it."

He had hoped it wouldn't come up, so he wouldn't have to tell him what he'd found. But it had, and he wasn't about to lie to Ike. "I checked the top of the cliff on the way over. I found footprints above the cave and a place where somebody rolled a big rock down the cliff."

Ike almost dropped the wrench. "I knew it! I just knew it! That's twice somebody has tried to kill us! We have to talk to our folks. It's just too dangerous."

"Maybe and maybe not."

"What does that mean?" Ike did not look happy, his face pinched together in a scowl. "First Whitey tries to cut my throat and then Fishbone tries to bury us alive, and you don't seem to think things have gotten out of hand?"

"No, I mean for one thing it wasn't Fishbone. He wears the same boots every day, and I know what his tracks look like. Besides the tracks were too big. Whoever it is, has enormous feet."

"Whitey. Big hands and big feet."

"What I can't figure out is how he knew we were going to be there?"

"He must have followed us. We were so busy looking at the ground for the old cart path that he could have followed us in a tank and we wouldn't have seen him."

Asa laughed.

"It's not funny, Asa. I'm scared and I don't mind saying it. Whitey has come down from The High Ground and he's watching us. He's probably watching us right now."

Asa stepped back out the door and picked up his twenty-two and his backpack. "I told my Mom we were going to shoot some tin cans," he said.

"You're scared too, but you just won't admit it!"

"Of course I'm scared. On the other hand, we've escaped him each time, and that has to worry him just a little. The question is why he's still after us. He must think we know something and he's afraid we'll get to the treasure before he does. Or maybe he's afraid we'll go to our folks."

"And that's just what we should do!"

"He's such a screwball that he probably believes in enchantments and ghosts. I thought maybe you could think of a way to make him think we have some kind of special powers. A trick of some kind."

"Not now."

Asa checked the gun again to make sure it was empty, and then leaned it against the inside wall of the boathouse. "Just forget about Whitey for a moment, okay. Look, last night Fishbone and Dad went out eeling, and while they were gone I searched the cabin and I found Fishbone's half of the map, and I made a copy."

"You did!"

"Yeah, but the map doesn't make any sense." Asa took the map and the charts from his backpack and spread them on the workbench by the window. "I mean, well, it says it's Kidd's Creek, but it doesn't resemble either the charts or Thompson's map."

Ike studied the three maps, going from one to the other, and then stood there scratching his head. "They're not the same all right, but at the same time they are." Suddenly he grinned, picked up Fishbone's map, flipped it over, and held it up to the window. "It's backward," he said.

"Ike, I always knew you were smart, but this beats everything. I'd never have seen that."

Ike picked up Thompson's map and held it over Fishbone's. "They fit perfectly," he said.

"So what's the matter with that?"

"What are the chances of two people making separate maps and having them fit?"

"Not too good, I'd guess."

"Where did you find the map?" Ike asked.

"What are you getting at?"

"Was it lying right out in the open or did you have to look for it? I mean, how hard was it to find?"

"He had taped it to the bottom of the table, but under the drawer."

Ike wiped his hands on a rag and looked back down at the maps. "Asa, something is bothering me here."

"What are you thinking about?"

"That maybe we're being set up somehow."

"But why?"

"I don't know why."

"Let me ask you something. Did you think Whitey was going to cut your throat?"

"Well, I did, and that's no lie."

"You're worried because the maps are the same, right?"

"Yup."

"What if Kidd asked Thompson for a map of the creek?"

"You mean maybe Thompson just traced his own map and gave a copy to Kidd." Ike frowned. "How old would you say the paper is on Fishbone's map?"

"I didn't think about it, but it isn't parchment. Probably not too old."

"That means," Ike said, "that there's an original somewhere, and Fishbone's map was copied from that original."

"Which means probably someone else will come looking, and that doesn't give us much time. If we go to our folks, they'll call in the cops and everything will come to a stop. Meanwhile, whoever has the original of the map is bound to start looking."

"Right." Ike pointed to the numbers written on the map. "What do you make of this?"

"Compass bearings I thought."

"That's what I think too." He turned, picked up a wide board, and crossed to the north window. "Bring the maps over here. Did you bring your compass?"

Asa dipped into his backpack. "Of course," he said and he opened the compass, and then gathered the maps and carried them to the makeshift table Ike had set up.

Carefully they oriented the maps to the compass. "It says sight through pin at 340, intersect 5 from tallest tree." Ike scratched his head. "What pin?"

"The one in the boulder at Boulder Bend? It's the only pin I know of."

"The Viking pin."

"Right."

"You think maybe Kidd drove that pin?"

"Whether he did or not, it's the only pin I know of." He set Fishbone's map on top of Josiah's and then oriented the compass from Boulder Bend. "Look, when you put the maps together the line runs right through that boulder. Kidd just left it off his map." He pointed to the map. "See, it goes right through it."

With a straight edge, Asa marked a line running at 340 degrees. "That gives us one line, but without a sight from that old tree we can't get an intersect."

Suddenly the wind picked up and Asa stepped outside, looking up at the quickly blackening sky. "No clamming today. It's fixing to blow like the devil."

"Shut the door!" Ike called. "The maps are blowing all over the place!"

Asa stepped back inside, closed the door, and helped Ike pick up the maps.

Ike unrolled their new chart and oriented it to north. Then he set the compass on the boulder and marked the line. "What we need to do is think this through. Gold is heavy which means they wouldn't have lugged it too far, and they didn't have much time." He looked at the chart and then at Thompson's map. "Suppose we took a guess." He tapped the edge of The High Ground with the pencil. "We left the boat right about here, wouldn't you say?"

"A little to the left. Remember the ledge? We were just to the left of that ledge."

"How do you know that's where the ledge was?"

"Because it's the same on all three maps. The creek may have changed where it could cut through the muck, but it couldn't cut away that ledge in three hundred years."

"Okay." Ike followed the edge of The High Ground with the pencil, hesitating and moving on. "Here," he said, "this is where I came out, and the old stump was almost straight above me, right about here." He marked a spot with the pencil, picked up the compass, marked the reading either side, and then drew a line connecting those two points and intersecting the line they had drawn through the pin. "Somewhere in here, wouldn't you think?"

"We wouldn't have to be off by much to be way off."

"What would you guess? A couple of hundred feet either way?"

"Seems right."

"So what we should do is take our machetes and a long stick, and run a survey line from Boulder Bend out to the edge of the first pond above Boulder Bend."

"We'll need a transit," Asa said.

"My uncle Jack is a surveyor, and he gave us one of his old ones a couple of years ago."

"Do you know how to use it?"

"He showed me."

"Okay," Asa said. "So we survey a line and then what?"

"Along that line we look for something unusual. It's certain that Kidd didn't dig a hole just anywhere in the marsh. He would have picked his spot carefully."

Asa smiled. "And we've got something he never figured on. Metal detectors."

Ike slapped his friend on the shoulder. "The metal detectors. Of course! Asa, we are going to find Kidd's treasure!"

Asa looked out the window again. "But not today, and anyway we got some planning to do. I don't think it'd be smart to cut a path from the edge of the creek. We ought to start in a way so nobody passing by would see the trail. And we need to make sure the transit is working, and then we have to gather our equipment, picks, and shovels, and ropes, and whatever else we can think of and ... and then we need to make sure that nobody is watching." He laughed. "We also need to stay out of sight. I made a deal with my mother that we'd go clothes shopping on the first rainy day."

Chapter 14

Foul Weather

Before the storm hit, Asa headed home. It was where you went when a big storm came. And this threatened to be a monster of a storm. A true nor'easter. A flat-out blow with the winds howling out of the northeast and the rain coming down in sheets so thick you couldn't see across the yard. And usually, Asa thought, he looked forward to days when the weather closed in because it kept his father home, spending most of the day in the shop, repairing broken tackle and mending nets. And when he worked he talked, rattling off the stories and adventures which had become the legends of the men who fished from King's Point.

But this day his father had gone out fishing, hoping to get in at least a few hours before the storm broke, and as a result Meg did not drag Asa down to King's Point to shop, as she had promised. With Tom at sea and a storm coming, she stayed close to the radio. Time after time she walked to the window to look out at the steadily blackening clouds, and each time she shook her head and returned to cleaning.

Asa tried reading, but not even Kenneth Roberts' *Arundel* could hold his attention, and finally he joined his mother, pacing between the kitchen and the windows in the front of the house. They kept the volume on the two-way radio turned up, the static cackling and spitting like grease on a hot stove, penetrating to every corner of the house, adding to the feeling of disquiet. The hours ticked by as slowly as they did when he was in school. The sky darkened steadily until they had to turn on the lights, but still the storm did not break over them, instead hanging in the sky like some monstrous wave. By eight in the morning Tom had been gone four hours.

Asa walked outside with Tar and stood where he could see the southeastern sky. The storm was coming up the coast so it would hit at sea first, and he wondered whether it already had. They weren't calling it a hurricane because the winds hadn't reached that speed, but it would still act like a hurricane, and any storm at sea was dangerous. At nine o'clock the first drops of rain burst from the low black clouds without warning. One second there was nothing and in the next he was running for the house in a downpour. Far off he could hear the rumble of thunder, and he ran just a little faster, leaping up onto the back porch, Tar right beside him.

He stood for several seconds watching the rain coming down so thick it was like watching a waterfall. Already the visibility had been cut in half, and it would get worse once the wind came up, but for now it was just the rain. He let Tar in and then walked into the kitchen and sat at the table. "Where was Dad going today?" he asked.

"Pine Point."

"Lots of good coves he could put into down that way," Asa said, trying to find some way to ease the tension, though he knew from the past that only when she heard Dad's voice on the radio would she relax. Until then all you could do was wait, and the longer you waited, the more likely it was that he'd run into trouble.

And then in an explosion of static the radio came alive. "*Shitepoke* to base, *Shitepoke* to base ... Meg?"

She grabbed the microphone and pushed the talk button. "Tom, where are you?"

"King's Point. Tried to call earlier, but with the weather I couldn't raise anybody. Storm's carrying a big static charge. Radio's are out clear to Portland. Meg, would you call Millie and tell her that Pete's here too. He's unloading or he would have called by land line."

"I'll call right away."

"Be two hours or so unloading and then we'll head upcreek. Gonna wait for the tide to come up so I don't have to worry about the channel with the visibility near gone. It'll be two, maybe three, time I get home."

"If you're later, call, okay?"

"I'll use a land line, but I expect to be on schedule."

Within seconds of the call, Asa returned to thoughts of Kidd's treasure. He climbed the stairs to his room and lay down on his bed, listening to the wind howling out of the storm, but it did not seem so strong now that he knew Dad was safe in harbor.

But exploring upcreek today would be useless. You couldn't take sightings when you couldn't see more than a few yards. Worse, it would be a very nasty wet ride up and back, and ... more to the point, his mother would not let him take the boat out in a storm like this. He lay on his bed listening to the rain beat against the house, now soft, now loud as the wind ebbed and flowed, and sometimes between gusts it sounded as if the storm had stopped to draw in a long breath. In those seconds the rain rapped only against the roof, and then the next gust came, driving the rain against the house, the force of it like water from a fire hose.

Today he did not want the rain and the gunmetal gray light made him restless and uneasy. He tried reading a book but the story could not hold his mind, and he drifted again and again to the maps, and Whitey, and Fishbone. Dad wouldn't get back till mid-afternoon, and he thought about exploring the cave. He didn't think Whitey would take to prowling around in this weather, but just to be on the safe side, he could take Tar and check the area for any sign. But that wouldn't work in the rain, he thought, because any scent would wash right away. The phone rang in the office and he heard his mother answer it. "Asa," she called, "it's Ike."

"Okay, thanks." He rolled quickly off the bed, jogged down the stairs to the office, and picked up the receiver.

"Asa. Do you think we can go?" Ike asked.

"What do you think?"

"Yeah, I know. We can't see anything, darn the luck."

"But I got another idea," Asa said, "Maybe we could explore the cave."

Ike hesitated. It seemed like something they could do anytime, but as long as they couldn't go upcreek it would be a good way to spend the afternoon. "Okay," he said, "but what do I tell my mother?"

"You say you're coming over here to help me get my engine working, and I'll say I'm going over to help you work on the old dory, and then we'll meet at the cave."

One thing about Asa, Ike thought, he always had a way to get around adults without arousing a whole lot of suspicion. Still he could see some trouble with this idea. "What if one of our Moms calls the other?"

"Heck, Ike, you gotta take some risks. And besides they won't go out in this weather to check the boathouses."

"Okay, that sounds right, but our dads will be in by three. Can we finish by then?"

"It's not all that big, Ike, it won't take us a half-hour."

"But maybe we'll find more cave once we have lights."

"How much bigger can it be?"

"I don't know, but there's a whole mountain there," Ike said. "And the other thing ... should I bring my rifle?"

"No, I wouldn't dare to fire a rifle in a cave, there's no telling where the bullet might bounce to."

"Jeez, Asa. I'm not an idiot, you know."

Asa did not answer and then he said, "I'm bringing my baseball bat."

"For batting bats?"

"Funny, Ike. Just remember who had the highest average this spring." He stopped. "You think there's bats?"

"Sure. All caves have bats."

"Maybe you better bring your bat too."

"Okay," Ike said. "It's eleven now. Eat early and we'll meet at the cave at quarter to twelve. And bring an extra flashlight and extra batteries."

Asa brought two flashlights, extra batteries, his compass, and his thirty-two inch aluminum baseball bat. And wearing his bright yellow rain jacket, pants, and rubber boots he walked along the dirt road toward Ike's. Once out of sight of the house he turned and cut off through the woods in a straight line for the cave. He liked walking out in the rain because of the way everything smelled so fresh and clean, and he liked the way the wind whipped the treetops and howled through the pines.

But when he came out of the woods by the cave, his mood changed, and he stood looking at the rock, blackened by the rain, and he felt uneasy about going back into the dark of the cave. There was no telling what they'd find but he was pretty sure they were going to see a lot more now that they had lights. He had not forgotten the emptiness in the pit of his stomach when the rocks had come tumbling down and sealed them in. It was the kind of thing you had nightmares about. In fact, it should have been enough to keep him from ever going into that cave again.

He looked around, turning his body because of the rain hood as Ike came out of the woods also dressed in yellow rain gear, the standard for all fisherman because you could be seen more easily if you fell overboard.

"You ready?" Ike asked.

"Sure."

"Let's go."

They climbed up the broken rocks to where they had dug their way out after the rock slide, and then stopped and stared at the entrance to the cave.

"Look at that," Ike said. "Someone else has been here."

The hole had been widened considerably, made large enough now to climb in easily, large enough even for a full grown man.

"Do you think someone's in there?" Asa asked.

"I don't know."

"Maybe we should forget about it."

Ike was not about to be put off that easily. "Naw, Com'on, Asa, nobody would be in there on a day like this. Probably somebody was just looking for Indian stuff and found where we had pulled the rocks away." Ike stepped into the hole, stopped, took out his three-cell light, and played the narrow beam from side-to-side. "Com'on ..."

Asa slipped down through the opening and pulled out his light. Slowly they worked their way down the jumbled rock inside to the floor of the cave. Some light came in from the hole above, and within a few steps the only light came from their flashlights.

"This is neat," Ike said as he flashed his light slowly over the walls and the ceiling. "Look at how dry it is, just like Josiah said."

Asa swept his light very slowly across the floor. "Footprints," he said.

They stopped and looked at the footprints in the soft dust. Big, size twelves, anyway, Asa thought, as he traced them with his light, running straight back into the cave. To the left he saw the footprints heading back out, and he turned and followed them back to the rocks. The dust which had stuck to the shoes had left a track back up and out of the cave, and he began to feel more comfortable.

"Looks like he left," Ike said.

Asa nodded. "That's what it looks like."

Ike shown his light upward toward the ceiling ten feet away and then to the walls either side. "It sure is bigger than I thought it was," he said.

Asa had begun to feel a good deal better. "Let's go."

The cave bent slightly to the right, and around the turn

they found storage shelves along the walls, empty now and covered with dust. Next they found some old wooden kegs, also empty, and then black smears here and there on the walls where torches had spread a carbon fan over the rock.

"Man, this is neat!" Ike said. "We can make this our headquarters."

And then with a great, high pitched squealing and a rush of wings, several hundred bats let go of the ceiling and swirled about them, flying out toward the opening, and then back, and then back to the opening again, and the boys ran deeper into the cave getting past the roost, and then behind them they could hear the bats settling down.

"What a lot of bats, huh?" Ike looked back the way they had come.

"I always wondered where all the bats lived."

"Mom says they eat their own weight in bugs every night. Maybe we shouldn't make this our headquarters so we don't chase the bats away. I like anything that eats mosquitoes."

"I don't like bats," Asa said.

They walked deeper into the cave, flashing their lights along the walls, and the ceiling, and the floor, and now the cave had narrowed to half its width, and they could even reach up and touch the ceiling. Asa thought his father could not have walked without bending over, and then within another ten feet the ceiling dipped lower, and Asa had to duck his head, though Ike made it through easily.

In the dust they could see where the man who had been there had crawled along the floor, and just as Asa began to worry about going any farther, they came to a solid wall. Ike flashed his light this way and that, but plainly they had come to the end of the cave. "Wow, I guess that's it," he said. "Not much to it, is there?"

"Not much," Asa said. "Com'on, let's go back."

But Ike continued to explore with his light, walking right up to the end wall, and then turning to look back out the way they had come, and in the flare of Asa's light he saw something unusual, stepped off to his left, and disappeared.

"Ike! Ike, where are you?"

Suddenly Ike appeared, smiling. "Look at this," he said. "Another passage. You can't see it from anywhere but with your back against the wall." He shown his light on the ground. "And whoever came in here before us didn't find it either. See, his footprints don't go anywhere near it."

They stepped around the rock wall and into another passage, and now they could stand upright, the ceiling two feet above their heads. Then the passage turned right, and they stepped through an opening the size of a doorway, and out into an open chamber twice the size of a house.

They stood close together, sweeping the lights over the walls and the ceiling, and then when the lights touched the floor they both jumped back, their hearts hammering, neither of them able to say a word. For across the floor of the cave lay bones, bones, and more bones, human bones, skeletons. Each one lay on its back, hands folded on the chest, row upon row half-buried in the dust. Cloth and leather still clung to some, and beside each skeleton lay arrows, bows, and knives, perfectly preserved in the dry air of the cave. And now they could hear a strange moaning, and it sounded as if someone were speaking to them.

"It's the spirits!" Ike said.

Chapter 15

A Close Shave

"Quiet!" Asa said.

They listened to the low, mournful sounds, trying to make them into words, but they could not.

"I'm getting out of here," Ike said.

"It's the wind, it must be the wind ..."

"No it isn't, Asa. It's the spirits Kidd mentioned."

"Ike, get a grip, will you? There's no such thing as spirits." He flashed his light over the rows and rows of skeletons. "This is the old burial ground we always heard about, only these aren't Indians. Look at those flint knives and axes. There's nothing like this in the museum. I read somewhere about an ancient people, a lot older than the Indians, but they all disappeared. I think this is where they buried their dead."

"Well they sure weren't alive," Ike said. "At least I hope they weren't."

Asa laughed. "Com'on, there's nothing here that can hurt you. Let's look around."

"I think we better get out of here!" said Ike, who was more than a little skittery on the subject of ghosts.

"As long as we don't touch anything, it's okay."

"Touch anything! Are you nuts? I wouldn't touch anything in here. The spirits would be after us in a second!"

"Jeez, Ike, are you really scared of spirits?"

"You're darn right I am. I'm shaking all over."

"If you want to go, go ahead. I want to look around."

Ike didn't move.

"Are you going?"

"N-not alone," he said.

Asa stepped to one side and shone his light up and down the rows of skeletons. Some were big and some small, and each one had either a weapon or a tool laid to its right side. "Ike," he said, "don't breath a word of this to anyone. We'll have to talk to our parents and make sure that they tell only the right people. Somebody from a museum maybe."

Suddenly the moaning stopped, and the boys stood and listened, but it did not start again.

"If we call a museum they'll come and take everything away, and that'll leave the spirits behind ... angry sp-spirits!" Ike ran the light up and down the rows again and again. "There must be two hundred skeletons in here. I'll bet nobody has ever seen anything like this before. I wonder how old they are." Slowly, Ike had begun to calm down.

Asa turned and flashed his light up against the wall behind them and stopped dead. "Ike," he said, his voice almost a whisper, "whatever you do, don't move an inch. There's a booby trap just over the entrance."

Ike turned to look up at an enormous boulder held in place by a single pole.

"There must be a trip wire." Asa flashed his light along the pole until he found a line dangling from one end, and then followed the line down the wall to where it disappeared beneath the dust of the cave floor. And now he saw the bump in the dust where the trip wire had extended across the entrance.

"That boulder is enormous," Ike said. "It would have crushed us like bugs."

"But it didn't work. Either we just got lucky and stepped over it, or the line rotted away over time and ..." He stopped the light on a footprint. One of then had stepped squarely on the raised mound. "Look at that!"

"Asa, I'm pretty scared," Ike said. "This place is full of evil spirits. I can feel them crawling in the air around me, watching me ...."

Asa laughed. "Ike, get hold of yourself. In all the stuff you've read about spirits, did you ever read about them hurting someone who meant them no harm?"

"I don't care. I want to get out of here!" He turned toward the entrance.

"Ike!" Asa shouted. "Whatever you do, don't you move! Promise me, you won't move. I have to make sure that this trip wire doesn't work. And there may be other wires that I can't see." He squatted down and studied the floor, but he couldn't see without brushing away the dust, and if he accidentally tripped something they would be trapped in the cave again. "How far can you jump?"

"Pretty far."

"Enough to clear that mound?"

"I think so."

"I'll move back into the cave, but if the rock lets go you'll be on the other side, and then you can go for help, okay?"

"Okay. No! Not okay. I'll be alone!"

"But you'll be outside this room, and the only scary thing in the rest of the cave is the bats."

"I don't care about bats."

"Then make the jump."

Ike looked up at the boulder and then at the distance he had to jump to clear the mound and land in the doorway to the outer cave. Six feet at least. That was a long way to jump but he couldn't see any other way. He tossed his baseball bat back through the tunnel, took off his rain parka and his rain pants, and tossed them well ahead into the tunnel. Then he took off his rubber boots as well. He crouched down and began swinging his arms back and forth, back and forth, building up momentum, trying to get every bit of energy into his legs. Suddenly, with a great outward blast of breath he hurled himself upward as his legs shot him forward. He cleared it easily, sailing over the mound and landing back inside the tunnel, and then something gave way beneath his feet and he heard a great crash behind as the boulder let go. "Asa! Asa!" he shouted as he dug a flashlight from his pocket. No answer. "Asa!" He flashed his light toward the opening but the dust hung thick in the air, and he called again, panicky now, and certain Asa must have been caught by the boulder. "Asa! Asa! Can you hear me?"

"Boo!"

Ike nearly leaped out of his pants he jumped so high, and he let out a squealing screech that would have shamed a stuck pig. "Asa! Don't scare me like that!"

"I'm sorry, Ike. I shouldn't have done that."

"How did you get out?"

"The boulder came down to one side. The trip line worked, but for some reason the boulder fell to the side and left me enough space to get through. There were two trips. The first one was meant to block the entrance, the second was meant to kill you if you got past the first."

Ike, fascinated with the mechanics of the trap began to forget his fear. "Which means there must be another entrance, or the Shamans would have had to pry the boulder loose from here, and it would be a lot easier to do that from inside." Suddenly he froze. "Asa! What was that!"

"What was what?"

A sharp noise echoed through the cave.

Asa whispered back. "Put your light out and pick up your bat." The dark snapped in on them, a dark as dark as the inside of an ink barrel, the kind of dark that exists where light does not shine. And they waited, listening, trying not to breathe. Something walking, the footsteps soft in the dust, but audible, and then suddenly the bats let go from the cave ceiling, and the boys flattened themselves against the wall. Then as the bats settled down, Asa heard the footsteps again, and then no sound at all, nothing until something cold and wet touched the back of his hand, and it was his turn to jump, knocking his head against the hard rock ceiling with a solid resounding thud, and then grabbing his head with both hands.

"Asa!" Ike shouted as he switched on his light and two big yellow eyes leaped out of the dark. He howled and jumped back, and then he laughed. "It's Tar, Asa, it's just Tar."

Asa rubbed his head and checked his hand for blood. No blood. Just a bump ... a big bump.

"You okay?" Ike asked.

"Uh-huh, just banged my head." He squatted down and Tar licked his ear. "Good old Tar," he said, "you about scared me to death."

"Now you know what it feels like, anyway."

"I'm sorry about scaring you, Ike."

"I'm getting a little tired of being scared," he said, and then he chuckled. "You can't believe how big Tar's eyes looked in the dark. All I could see was huge, glowing eyes."

They laughed as they relaxed and began to gather their wits. "Ike, can you believe this? All that stuff about Indian graves on The High Ground and they turn up in our own backyard. You want to have another look?"

"Yeah."

"You sure you're okay on the spirits?"

"Sure. I'm okay on that now. Especially with Tar here. Dogs can sense stuff like that long before we can."

They stepped back into the passageway and then into the burial chamber as Tar stopped dead in his tracks. "Tar, stay!" Asa said.

Ike flashed his light around the walls of the chamber. "Asa, you know what's odd? Out in the other part of the cave you can see where the torches smoked up the walls, but here there's nothing like that. What did they use for light?"

"I don't know. Maybe the shamans never left the cave and they got so they could see in the dark. Or maybe on bright days there's a faint light in here from the other entrance." He stepped back to the doorway. "If you stand still, you can feel the wind from the outer cave. Maybe it'll feel the same way at the other entrance. Or maybe it'll make a sound because of the high wind outside." Slowly, he started down along the cave wall, keeping to the pathway between the wall and the rows of bones. They walked under an overhang until the wall curved, and then they stopped and shone their lights upward toward the high arch of the ceiling.

"Wow," Ike said, "Look at that." He held his light against a giant sun carved into the rock ceiling. "How do you suppose they got up there to do that?"

"They must have known how to build a scaffold," Asa said. "Or maybe they made a net of some kind."

"Do you hear that?" Ike asked.

"Hear what? All I can hear is the wind."

"Pretty eerie," Ike said. "Like someone breathing...."

"Jeez, Ike, don't say things like that. You're making me scared now."

"But it does. Listen ..."

They stood, looking up toward the ceiling, their lights aimed at the great sun carved into the stone, and they could hear the wind outside. At times it roared lion loud and at others it seemed to purr like a kitten. But now they knew it was the wind, and it sounded nothing like the moaning sounds they had heard before.

"Turn out your light," Asa said.

"Are y-you nuts!"

"No, it's okay. Honest."

"I'm not turning out my light, Asa!"

"Com'on Ike, there's nothing here that can hurt you."

"Okay, okay, but just for a second."

At first the dark slammed in so hard and dense that unless you put a hand against the wall of the cave you could not tell whether you still stood upright. But then, almost as if someone were slowly, very slowly turning a dimmer switch, a soft glow from above began to push back the dark.

"The light comes right through where they carved the sun," Asa said. "I'll bet when the sun's out it's bright as day."

"Can light go through rock?" Ike asked.

"Yeah. I read about it in a building somewhere."

"Would the Indians have known how to do that?"

"I don't think they were Indians," Asa said.

In the dim light they could make out the rows of skeletons, but they could see little detail, and finally Ike switched on his light, playing the beam on the bones which lay nearby. "Hey, Asa, look at that one. He must have been killed in battle. He's got a hole right in the middle of his forehead."

"Must have given him some headache, huh?"

The boys chuckled as they looked at the skeletons, talking about them, gaining courage, and then suddenly they stopped talking and turned toward the doorway.

"Did you hear that?" Asa whispered.

"Yeah. I heard it," Ike whispered back. "It sounded like a rock falling."

Just then Tar growled, barked, and ran through the doorway into the outer cave. Ike picked an aisle between the skeletons, and the boys crossed to the doorway and picked up their baseball bats, and then they heard the bats let go, and Tar began to bark louder, the way he barked when something had aroused his anger.

But even as they stepped into the main cave they could not tell where the barking came from. Ike was standing directly behind Asa, flashing his light off to the left as Asa flashed his ahead. Suddenly the beam from his light shone directly into the face of a large black bear standing on its hind legs twenty feet away. "WHOA!" Asa shouted and leaped backward into Ike, knocking him tail over teakettle.

"What the heck?" Ike's rain hood had fallen over his face, and he'd dropped his light and he couldn't see a thing.

"Run! It's a bear!" Asa shouted over Tar's barking, and he turned and ran into Ike just as he was getting to his feet, and both of them sprawled into the dust on the cave floor.

"Asa! Stop knocking me over!"

The bear, already pretty edgy over having to keep Tar at bay was as badly startled as Asa, and he dropped onto all four feet and legged it for the front of the cave with Tar right on his heels, barking and growling, but keeping his distance as long as the bear was headed away from Asa and Ike.

"A bear! A big bear!" Asa shouted as he got to his feet.

"A bear?" Ike flashed the beam of his light on the rump of the rapidly retreating bear. "That's all? Just a bear?"

"I don't like bears, Ike. I never liked bears!"

"Call Tar," Ike said.

"What?" Asa was absolutely addled.

"Call Tar before he tangles with the bear."

"Tar! Come!" Asa shouted as both he and Ike ran after the bear and the dog. "Tar! Come!"

All the activity had made the bats most unhappy, and they went chirping and squealing and fluttering through the dark, but now all Asa could think about was Tar getting too close to the bear, and he called him again as he ran, the bats banging into his arms and bouncing off his slicker, and then he heard the clatter of claws as the bear scrambled up the rocks, and when he flashed his light he could see Tar standing at the base of the rock pile, watching the bear digging on up the rocks and then scurrying through the hole and out into the storm.

Asa dropped to the floor of the cave next to Tar, looping an arm around Tar's thick neck and rubbing his ears. "Good, boy," he said. "You showed that old bear."

The bats had begun to settle, and Ike came up and sat down next to Asa and Tar. "This is the craziest day ever," Ike said as he chuckled. "But the craziest thing of all is that I finally found something you're scared of."

"I'm scared of lots of things," Asa said, "but I am a whole lot scared of bears."

"They're harmless, Asa."

"Says who?"

"Says me and everybody else. The only time they're dangerous is when they have cubs."

"I'm not changing my mind."

Ike laughed. "If someone had told me that Asa Clark was scared of bears, I'd have called him a liar."

"The only good thing about bears is that you don't see 'em very often."

"I'd rather be scared of bears," Ike said. "At least you *can* see 'em."

"I didn't know you were scared of ghosts," Asa said.

"Well, I am."

"Hey, I didn't mean to hurt your feelings, Ike."

"I'm just a little touchy about it," Ike said.

"Like me and bears."

"Yeah, I guess so."

Suddenly Asa felt more tired than he could ever remember. "I don't know about you, but I'm ready to go home."

"Should we tell our folks?"

"Not right away."

"Because of the maps."

"If we tell them about the cave, then we'll have to show them, and we'll never get back upcreek."

"I don't guess the skeletons will go anywhere," Ike said.

"I don't suppose."

"Do you think we ought to go back to the end of the cave and brush away all the footprints just in case Whitey comes back."

"I don't think he'll come back," Asa said. "In a way it's too bad he didn't find it. With those great big feet, he'd have been sure to have set off the trap."

"I could have lived with that," Ike said.

They both laughed, and then scrambled up the rocks and out into the rain and the wind, Tar dashing on ahead, his nose glued to the bear tracks they couldn't see.

"Can you imagine being able to smell what Tar smells?" Ike asked.

Asa grinned. "I don't think I'd want to spend much time putting my nose where he puts his."

Chapter 16

A Surprising Discovery

Asa sat in the stern, running the engine, steering the boat upcreek through the tatters of the fog, now giving way rapidly to the summer sun. He was so consumed by anticipating what lay ahead that his knees rattled like the legs of a frightened rabbit. He thought he had never done anything even half so exciting. Kidd's treasure! They would all be rich and they would go down in history. As long as they got to the treasure first. And that had suddenly got a lot more complicated this morning when Fishbone turned up missing. He'd been there at night and in the morning he was gone, seabag and everything.

His father had thought it particularly odd that he had chosen to walk the ten miles into town, and even stranger that he'd left without getting paid, but he'd dealt with such men long enough to know that you could never count on them for long, and he'd just shrugged it off. But Asa knew where Fishbone was headed, and it wasn't for town. He was headed for The High Ground to meet Whitey.

Ike sat facing forward, eager to be there, to get started, and he wondered whether Fishbone and Whitey were watching them even now. From The High Ground you could see the whole creek, and anyone sitting in a tree with binoculars would know where they stopped.

As they came around the bend by the rope swing a snowy egret leaped up from the shore and sailed out over the marsh, and Ike's heart skipped as the memory of his dream flooded his mind. But the bird only circled lazily, pumping its wings in a slow, steady rhythm and then dropped back down behind the boat. Just an egret like all the egrets on the creek, startled by the boat, but not wanting to give up its fishing ground.

At the next bend another egret came up, and it followed the same pattern, swinging out over the marsh and then dropping in behind as the creek returned to normal. All the same, seeing the birds just now made the dream seem real, and then he thought about Whitey and Fishbone, and he was doubly glad they had brought their rifles along.

Each bend produced another bird, and finally he turned and faced Asa, and at first that made him feel a good deal more comfortable. Looking out over the white wake of the boat against the blue water he watched the egrets fade into the distance as they looped out over the marsh and settled back along the edges of the creek. Why were the birds making him so uneasy? Because of the dream? Probably. No. It wasn't the dream. The birds were like flags. Anyone watching would see them go up and then down, and they would know a boat was coming upcreek even if they couldn't see it. He waved his hands at Asa to slow, and when the sound of the motor dropped, he leaned toward the stern. "Asa, the egrets! They're giving us away. We have to get there faster."

Asa watched another bird sail past. "Okay, but keep a sharp watch. If I shear a pin we'll be forever getting there."

Ike turned in his seat and hung out over the bow as Asa cranked the throttle to full speed and the skiff broke into a plane, riding up onto the water and flattening out. So many thoughts crowded into his mind now that he found it hard to focus but he pushed each thought aside as he watched for rocks or stumps or anything that stuck up far enough from the bottom to catch the propeller. It was unlikely they'd hit anything. The water here was deep, the tide was at least halfway to high, and slowly he lost track of the time. The next thing he knew, Asa had throttled back the engine and brought the boat toward shore. Slowly, with the water getting steadily shallower, he sidled the boat up against the bank.

Ike stepped out into the knee-deep water and carried the anchor far enough to hold the boat just downstream of the enormous boulder. Hidden there in the lee of the boulder it could not be seen from The High Ground.

"You ready?" Asa asked as he stepped out of the boat and handed the transit to Ike. "Need some help?"

"I practiced setting it up last night."

"Don't forget to cover yourself with the camo net before you stand up."

"I'm not stupid, Asa."

"Sorry, just being careful." He took his machete, two stiff bamboo poles, and a short crowbar from the boat. Then he walked upstream a short way and tucked back into the reeds to wait for Ike to set up the transit. He seemed to take forever getting the tripod spread, and then he had to level the platform and make sure the pointed brass plumb hung directly over the iron pin in the rock.

It made a comical sight, Asa thought, as he looked at the camouflaged lump which had suddenly appeared on top of the rock, and while it would fool no one close up, the net would work well at a distance.

Ike waved his hands to signal that he was ready, and Asa moved back into the reeds a few feet and held up the pole. Then he moved it back and forth until Ike signaled for him to hold. He used the crowbar to stab a hole into the ground, stuck the pole into it, and then stamped the soil in around the base. He waited for Ike to check the line.

With the first pole set, he backed through the reeds, trying to maintain as straight a line as he could. Then he held up the second pole, surprised at how far off line he had gone. When it was set, he used the machete to cut a path to the first pole, pulled it free, and carried it out to the second pole. Once again he backed out into the marsh, checking over his shoulder with each step to make sure he didn't disappear down some hole.

He set the pole on the line as Ike directed him, and then he cleared back to the other pole. No one traveling the creek could see where the path began because of the reed wall they had left standing by the edge of the creek. When he had completed the path between the poles he retrieved the pole, set it beyond the end of the path, and cleared the reeds away. Then he returned to the boat to help Ike with the rest of the gear.

From then on they sighted and chopped, sighted and chopped, and lugged gear until they reached the shore of the fingernail pond. Tired and hungry and hot, they decided to wash away the sweat with a quick swim and then eat while they considered their next step.

Sitting in the shade of the reeds they looked back down the path. Flat. Absolutely flat. Not a bump, not a rock, not a ripple in the land for as far as they could see. Just flat.

"I guess we better look at the maps again," Ike said.

"Not much else to do," Asa said.

"Where do you think we went wrong?"

"I don't know."

"Could it be on the other side of the pond?"

Asa opened his backpack and pulled out the maps. "According to the map, this pond was part of the main creek then. With a boat, it wouldn't have been much trouble to bury the gold over there."

"That would have been on the outside bend and the water would have been deepest there," Ike said.

"But on a high tide they could put in here."

"It's gotta be on this side," Ike said. "He wouldn't have buried it on the side where people were most likely to travel."

"Good thinking, Ike. Good thinking." Asa stood up and walked out to the shore of the pond and when he turned he saw the patch of feathery phragmities blowing in the breeze. There it was. High ground, some kind of high ground because that's the only place the phragmities grew. "Ike, Ike," he called. "Look! Over there! Phragmities!"

They pushed their way quickly through the reeds to where the ground gathered itself into a low knoll. The phragmities grew at the edges, but as the land rose, low growing grasses took over, and they stood looking at an elongated, rounded knoll maybe a hundred yards by thirty feet cov-

ered with rich green, ankle deep grass. It looked as if someone had buried some gigantic prehistoric whale.

Ike took out his compass, flipped up the clear rectangu-
lar line-of-sight window and tried to run a line from where
he thought the old tree must have stood. "I don't know how
close I can get," he said.

"Just do the best you can. The metal detector should do
the rest. But we'd better put on the camo shirts and pants
and hats. Anyone on The High Ground can see us clearly
now."

They started back and suddenly Ike grabbed Asa's arm
and pulled him aside. "Asa! Look out!"

"What?"

"Sink hole. Isn't that a sink hole?" He pointed to a low
spot just off the edge of the knoll. It looked harmless, just a
patch of dark earth covered with a light thatch of dead reeds.

"God, Ike, I'd have stepped right into it. Lucky we
haven't all lost our heads over this."

"I just happened to look over. I didn't know if it would
be as bad as the one when we were clamming, but if it was,
Asa, I could never have got you out." He shook his head.
"But now I know why people fall into them. They don't look
like anything, and the dead reeds hide them almost perfectly."

"How did you spot it?"

"You said nothing was growing on the one you stepped
in, and when I looked down I suddenly remembered that."

Asa shook his head. "And you're supposed to be the
one who goes all woolly in the head."

Ike laughed. "I do," he said. "You can't believe the hor-
rible things I've imagined since we started out."

"Well, at least we know where it is," Asa said. "And there

are probably others around too. We'll just have to watch where we step."

They walked to their gear, changed clothes, and brought back the shovel, the pick, and the metal detector and both rifles, which they laid carefully in the grass at the base of the mound.

While Asa tuned the dials on the machine, Ike took several compass readings. From here, looking back at the path they had cut, he could see where they had gone awry, and he adjusted the line and then dropped the shovel to mark the spot. Then he turned toward The High Ground, and guiding on a large old oak he marked off the distance to where he thought the stump stood, and then turned the compass to north and read the line. He was off. The intersect point had to be farther up on the mound. He walked ten feet, took a reading and kept at it until he could get the two lines to intersect. "Asa, best I can say, it must be somewhere in here." He swept his hand through the air to indicate a patch of ground. "But if I'm off a little then I'm off by a lot."

Asa walked up to the top of the mound and began sweeping the detector back and forth as he walked north. Then he turned, stepped three feet to his right, and came back heading south. Time after time he swept the area and then he swept it again from east to west. Nothing. Not a peep from the machine.

"Your battery okay?" Ike asked.

"I put in a new one."

"Are you sure the machine's working?"

Asa pulled out his pocket knife, tossed it into the grass, and swept the circular head of the detector over it. The sound came up at once and he saw the needle jump. "Nothing to do," he said as he picked up his knife, "but start at the beginning." He walked to where he had stopped before and started down the mound toward the path. Ten steps later the machine began beeping. He swept to the left, the right, and then ahead and each time got a strong reading. "This is it, Ike! Unless somebody buried an old car up here, this is it!"

He set the machine aside and Ike brought the pick and shovel. It was easy digging, nothing but sand and gravel and just as they reached the three foot mark Ike drove his pick and it struck the metal box with a dull ringing sound.

"Looks like the little pigses has found it," Whitey said. They whirled, looking into the barrels of two revolvers, one held by Whitey and the other by Fishbone.

"You boys just keep right to your digging," Fishbone said. "Hate to bother anybody what's doing hard labor." He laughed and the sound snarled up out of his raspy throat.

Asa looked into his eyes, but there was no sign of recognition. It was as if Fishbone had never seen him before and the eyes were cold and vicious. There was nothing to do but go to work. But they worked as slowly as they could, trying to gain time. They cleared the top of the big iron box and then began digging along the sides, Asa using the pick to loosen the dirt as Ike shoveled it into a pile.

"Too slow! Faster! Dig faster!" Whitey shouted.

"Leave 'em be," Fishbone said as he moved around to the downhill side of the hole. "They'll get it out of there soon enough. And this way they got longer to think about what it is we're going to do with 'em."

Try as he might, Asa could not get a good, front view of Fishbone's revolver. Had he reloaded it? Or was it still empty? It'd be nice to know that just now, he thought, because it would only leave them one gun to deal with, though even without his gun, Fishbone had them both overmatched. Asa measured the distance with his eye. If he were another foot closer he could hit him in the legs with the pick, but if he saw it coming he'd just jump out of the way.

They cleared the dirt from the ends so they could reach the handles, grabbed hold, and tried to lift it out. But no matter how hard they strained, they could not budge the chest.

"It's too heavy," Asa said. "We'll need help."

"Dig it out more. There ain't enough room in that hole," Fishbone said as he waved the revolver about.

"Be quicks, little weasels, be quicks!" Whitey said, his voice hushed and dangerous sounding.

They dug outward from the box a couple of feet, and then slowly dug down, taking their time, scooping out small shovel loads of gravel and sand, hoping Fishbone's patience would hold long enough for them to figure out what to do.

And then suddenly the hole had grown wide enough and Ike and Asa stood back as Fishbone tucked his revolver into his belt and stepped into the hole. "I'll take one end, you two take the other," he said.

At first the wet earth beneath the box seemed to suck it back down, and then Fishbone's shoulders bulged. He grunted loudly and as the box came free, they swung it up onto the ground outside the hole. "You boys stay right there," Fishbone said, as he stepped out of the hole. "We'll have to widen it a little, but it'll make a proper enough grave." He took out his revolver, stepped back as if to shoot away the rusty lock, and then suddenly he raised the barrel, pointed it at Whitey, and pulled the trigger. Nothing. He pulled the trigger again and again and each time the hammer cracked down on an empty chamber, and then Whitey reacted, raising his gun and firing directly into the middle of Fishbone's chest. Ike and Asa ducked into the hole as the revolver went off, wincing at the blast from the big forty-four so close. The force of the bullet threw Fishbone backwards down the incline and he fell spread-eagled on the sinkhole. "Kill old Whitey was his game, Fishbone who was Whitey's friend."

Then the body began to sink, and once it started it seemed to disappear almost all at once. Within seconds, the remains of Fishbone Watson were gone, and all that was left to mark his passing was a bare spot on the surface of the sinkhole and the lingering smell of gun smoke in the still air.

Whitey watched in disbelief, and then he stepped past the box, looking at the sinkhole as if to be certain of what he'd seen, and in the second he took his eyes off them, Ike cut loose his diving hawk imitation, the sound so loud and close that Whitey ducked out of instinct.

Asa took his only chance, swinging the pick with the same power he put into a baseball bat. The point of the pick caught Whitey in the middle of his back and went right though his body and out through his chest. For a second Whitey stood, his hands at his sides, and then the gun fell from his hand and he curled his fingers around the bloody point of the pick where it stuck from his chest. He looked around at Asa and then back at the pick, his pink eyes wide, his mouth open. "Whitey's been kilt," he said, " he's been kilt by boys ..."

His knees buckled and he staggered forward, his weight pulling him down the incline to fall face down in the sink hole. They did not know whether he was alive or dead when he disappeared.

For what seemed like a long time they just stood looking at the sink hole, stunned by what had happened, and by
the speed with which it had happened. Finally Ike shook his
head and looked around at Asa. "I don't believe it! You killed
him!"

"I didn't mean to ..." Asa sat down on the chest.

"No," Ike said. "I didn't mean it that way. I meant you
saved our lives. You saw what he did to Fishbone and we
were next."

"I still wish I hadn't killed him, though," Asa said.

"I don't know what to say," Ike said, "except that I'd
have done the same thing if I'd got the chance."

"I can't believe how fast they went down," Asa said.
"It's almost like they were never even here."

Never had Ike really understood what it might be like
to see someone die, and he decided that it was not something he ever wanted to see again. But he couldn't think of
anything to say to help Asa. "You didn't have any choice,
Asa."

Asa nodded. "It's okay," he said. "I had to do it and I
did it. I didn't have much time to think about it."

"I wonder how deep that hole is?"

Asa shivered, took a deep breath, and looked away from
the mud. "That was slick, remembering to use your hawk
imitation. What made you think of it?"

Ike pointed off toward The High Ground where a red
tail hawk circled lazily above the trees. "I saw him out of the
corner of my eye," he said.

"Well, that was what saved us, because without that I
wouldn't have had a chance."

"I think we got lucky too. I think we'd have had a lot

more trouble with Fishbone."

"Wasn't all luck," Asa said. "When I searched his cabin I found the pistol and took the cartridges out of it. But I didn't know till he pulled the trigger whether he'd reloaded it."

"What was it you said? 'If you're ready for something bad to happen you can save yourself'."

"I said that?"

"You did."

"Didn't think I was that smart."

"Asa?"

"Yeah?"

"Could we open the chest now?"

Asa grinned. "Would you believe I forgot it was there?" He stood up, grabbed the short crowbar, shoved the point into the lock, and popped it open. Ike pulled it away and they pushed back the lid.

"What is it?" Asa asked.

"Kidd's joke, I'd guess," Ike said. "Looks like pig iron." He picked up a bar, took out his knife and scratched across the rusted surface. "Yup. Pig iron. I thought the box felt kind of light once we got it out of the mud."

"But why would he have buried a chest full of pig iron?"

"Maybe there never was any gold?" Ike said.

Asa looked over at the sink hole. Had he really done that? Had he really killed someone? Had he really driven a pick right through him? It had all happened so fast, that without the bodies there, it didn't seem real. It was more like a scene from a movie.

"Asa, you okay?"

"I don't know."

Ike looked down at the sinkhole. "You didn't have any

choice. If you hadn't killed him he'd have shot us and thrown us into the sink hole."

"I keep thinking maybe there was another way."

"Suppose you'd knocked him out, and we'd tied him up and went and got the police. If they couldn't get Fishbone's body out of the sinkhole, they'd have no way to prove Whitey had killed anyone, and he wouldn't even have gone to jail, and he would have come looking for us."

"It isn't like it is in the movies," Asa said.

"In the movies the chest would have been full of gold," Ike said. "We'd be heroes ... we'd be rich heroes."

"Instead," Asa said, "we've got two bodies sinking deeper and deeper into the mud and a chest full of pig iron."

"We've still got a mystery," Ike said. "Because Kidd went to too much trouble just for a practical joke. I think the gold is here somewhere. I bet he buried this chest just to confuse the crew on his ship."

Asa's eyes suddenly grew very wide. "Josiah Thompson said the pig iron was stored in the cave and that Kidd stayed in the cave to make sure it was all properly stowed. And while they were hauling all that stuff to the cave, Kidd stayed there. Ike, that's where he buried the gold!"

"And that's how he knew about the cave spirits!"

"And that gives us a place to start looking."

Chapter 17

Down Creek To Home

The tide had dropped and they had to pole the boat out into the deeper water, both of them now thinking a lot less about Kidd's treasure than about the two men probably lost forever in the sink hole. Asa sat down, shipped his oar, and sat for several seconds looking at the motor, trying to decide whether he had enough energy to pull the starter cord. Ike, standing in the bow, poled the boat out into the current.

Asa watched the water sliding along and then he reached back for the motor, using it as a rudder to steer the boat down the tide without wasting gas.

"Do you think they'll ever find them?" Ike asked.

"How deep can a hole like that be?" Asa asked.

Ike shrugged. "At least they'll know where to look."

"Do you think they'll charge me with murder?"

Ike looked stunned. "Murder? It was self-defense."

"You see some funny stuff in the papers."

"I'll bet anything both of them have been in jail before. You'll be a hero!"

"Sure don't feel like one. I almost puked."

"Asa, you gotta get hold of yourself here. Whitey was just about to shoot when you hit him with the pick. If you'd waited a second longer, for sure one of us would be dead. No matter how bad you feel, think about that."

The truth was, he hadn't really thought about that. He had, but he hadn't. All he could see was the pick sinking into Whitey's back and then watching him fall into the sink hole, and that was what made it all so strange. It was like it had never happened. "I wish we could just leave them there."

"I don't," Ike said. "I want 'em pulled out and taken someplace far away and buried."

"What do you think will happen?"

Ike shrugged. "I guess the cops'll come and look for the bodies, and that'll be the end of it."

"What about the newspapers? I don't want to be famous for killing someone."

"But nobody will see it that way. You'll be a hero. If anything you oughta be mad. Jeez, Asa, those guys tried to kill us and steal Kidd's treasure! All you did was make the world a lot safer for everyone. Can you imagine what might have happened if they'd gotten away?"

Asa reached for the starter cord on the motor. "Maybe we oughta get this over with." The engine started on the first pull, and with plenty of water under the keel they headed downcreek, startling the egrets each time they came round a bend, and then suddenly Asa killed the motor. "If we tell our folks now, we won't get back to the cave for days."

"But if we wait, maybe the bodies will sink so deep they

can't be found. And then what?"

"I don't care, Ike, right now I want to search the cave."

"It'll be hard to explain, won't it?"

"I still don't care."

"But that's the problem, Asa. It'll look like we didn't care about two guys getting killed."

"We didn't do anything wrong, Ike. But if we tell about it now, then the cops'll come. This might be our only chance for days and days and days."

Ike gave in. "Okay," he said. "But let's make it fast."

"Okay." Asa started the engine, straightened the boat, and once he was sure it was in the channel, he opened it up. The boat leaped forward into a full plane.

But just where Kidd might have buried the gold in the cave, proved puzzling. Using the metal detector, they scanned the floor of the cave but turned up only odd bits of metal and one old cutlass broken off a foot from the handle.

"Only one place left to look," Asa said.

"Not much choice, is there." Ike looked over his shoulder in the direction of the burial chamber.

"That's where it is, Ike. I keep forgetting he knew about the cave spirits."

"So you *do* think there are spirits." Ike sounded as if he were ready to fly for home.

"There are no spirits. It's just the wind."

Ike was unconvinced. "I still don't like it," he said.

"We don't have any choice. It's the last place to look. We have to try," Asa said.

Ike tried as brave a grin as he could manage. "If nothing else, it'll let the poor bats calm down for awhile."

Carrying propane lanterns, the digging tools, and the metal detector, they walked to the back of the cave, and then stepped around the wall and into the chamber. They stopped and turned off the lanterns.

"Just like we thought," Ike said. "Look at this. It's almost as bright as day."

"It's amazing," Asa shook his head. "If anybody told me this, I'd never believe him."

For several minutes they looked around the huge chamber. "I didn't think it was so big," Ike said.

"Me neither. I'll bet there's five hundred skeletons."

"Kinda quiet." Ike's eyes had grown to owl size.

"That's cause there's no wind blowing. I told you it was just the wind." No sooner had he said that than a low moan began to rise, growing louder and louder and then suddenly tapering off. Ike whirled toward the door, and Asa grabbed him by the arm. "Ike, wait! We can't quit now!"

"Asa ... I'm scared and I don't mind saying it. I'm so sc-scared my bones are rattling like Bobby Kelly's snare drum."

"Get hold of yourself, Ike!" He grabbed his friend by the shoulders with both hands. "We have got to find out!"

And then as suddenly as it had started, the moaning stopped. "You okay?" Asa asked.

"I ... I don't know ..."

"Ike, if you run out on me now and I find the treasure, I'm keeping the whole thing."

"That's, th-that's not fair!"

"I need your help, do you understand?"

"Yeah." He glanced around, shifting his head from side to side. "If they'll just shut up, I'll be okay."

Asa let go of his shoulders and looked around, his eyes

sweeping the enormous chamber. "We need to narrow things down. You've read more about Kidd than I have. What kind of a man was he?"

"Tricky, clever. Never missed anything."

"Look around. Look for anything out of place," Asa said. "Would he have disturbed the skeletons?"

With something to think about, Ike began to recover. "What, Captain Kidd? He'd have dug up his mother's grave if he thought it was a good place to bury treasure."

"Then look at each skeleton. See the way they're laid out. The knives go to one side, tools to the other. And they're placed so that if the hands were put down to the sides they would just reach them."

"Okay ..." Ike stopped. "Asa, I do see one thing."

"What?"

"Every skeleton has its hands crossed on its chest except that one." He pointed to one two rows to the left of where they stood. "Maybe Kidd left that as a mark."

"We'll have to move the bones to find out."

"What about the metal detector?"

"Jeesh, talk about dumb." Asa picked up the machine, switched it on, adjusted the dials, and began walking down the row, slowly sweeping back and forth, and when he reached the skeleton with its hand by its side the beeper sounded clearly. He swept the head of the detector back and forth to find out how large an area it read. "There's something here, Ike, something big. Bring the shovel." Asa took off his earphones. "It's at least a couple of feet square, maybe bigger."

"I hate to move the bones," Ike said.

"Try digging in the aisle and then in."

Minutes later the shovel blade struck against metal. They dropped to their knees and scooped the dirt away with their hands to reveal another iron box, this one in perfect condition with not a sign of rust.

Carefully, they grabbed the handle and tried to pull it out from under the skeleton without collapsing the dirt above. The box did not move. "This chest is a whole lot heavier than the other," Ike said.

"Sure is," Asa said. "We'll have to dig a space ahead of it, then maybe we can slide it out."

They began digging a hole longer than the chest and slightly deeper so the chest could move downhill.

"What do you think?" Ike asked.

"I think we can slide it in this dry dirt. You ready?"

They wrapped their hands around the iron handle. "Together, Ike. One ... two .. .three ... heave!" The box moved less than an inch but the movement shook the skeleton above and the moaning started, loud this time, almost a wail and Ike leaped up, ready to run as Asa grabbed his leg.

"Let me go!" Ike shouted.

"No! If Kidd could stand it so can we!" He held tightly to Ike's leg, using every bit of his strength. "We have to shove dirt back under the bones to keep them from moving. Ike! Do you hear me?"

"I gotta get out of here!"

"Ike, so help me, I'll cut you out of the treasure and then I'll go down to Bousquet's and buy the fanciest dirt bike they got, and you'll have to sit around and watch me having all the fun." He could feel Ike begin to relax.

"Would you really do that?"

"You can count on it!" Asa felt the muscles in Ike's leg

relax, but he held on, wishing the moaning would just stop. "Damn, Ike, you were always the one who believed the treasure was here, and now we're just inches away."

"Okay. Okay, I'll try."

Asa let go. "Com'on," he said. "Pack dirt under the bones. Maybe if they don't move it'll quiet the spirits."

"Ha! I knew it! You do believe in the spirits!"

"I told you I hear the sound, but nothing is going to get in my way here, Ike."

"How are we gonna move the chest?" Ike asked.

"Maybe we could use rollers of some kind? Look around for some short round sticks. I'll keep digging."

"Where would I find rollers?"

"I don't know, Ike, just look."

Asa used his pocket knife to loosen the dirt along one edge of the chest before scooping it out with his hand. The process was slow, but he worked steadily.

"How you doing?" Ike asked.

"Did you find anything?"

"Sure. The old pole that held up the boulder." He handed Asa a piece of the pole.

"How'd you cut it?"

"I didn't. It broke into pieces when the boulder came down. Will they fit?"

Asa eased the stick under the box, working it back to the halfway point. "Perfect," he said. "Got two more?"

Ike handed him another and then another.

Asa lay on his stomach and reached back beyond the last roller, digging the dirt away until he felt the box begin to settle onto the stick. Then he switched to the other side.

"Ike, start packing the dirt back behind the box. We'll

make it nice and solid underneath the skeleton."

Ike pushed the dirt back behind the chest on his side, packing it carefully. As they worked, the moaning grew quieter. "It's working, I think it's working," Ike said.

Asa stood up. "Okay, let's try moving it again." They grabbed onto the handle and heaved, and this time the box moved several inches. They stopped to pack dirt behind it, then pulled on the handle again. Inch by inch they dragged the chest out from under the skeleton, carefully filling in the dirt beneath the bones, packing it tightly as they went, until the chest sat in the hole in the aisle and the skeleton once again lay on solid ground.

"Listen," Ike said. "They've stopped." In the quiet of the cave he could hear his heart beating. "Asa?"

"Yeah?"

"If you believe in the spirits, how come you didn't run?"

He shook his head. "I'm just greedier than you are."

Ike laughed. "Or a whole lot braver."

"You're still here, aren't you?"

"Only 'cause you wouldn't let go of my leg."

"You're braver if you're scared and you still stay." Asa slapped the chest. "We ought to get this open."

"Maybe we should drag it out to the entrance," Ike said. "I don't want to risk disturbing another skeleton."

"It's too heavy. We'll be at it the rest of the day. We can open it here. We'll just be real careful."

But this lock did not promise to give way as easily as the one in the marsh. There was not the least sign of rust, and when they pulled on it, the metal sounded hard.

"We should try not to destroy the lock," Ike said. "It's a museum piece. Especially since it's preserved so well. Probably worth a lot of money." He took out his pocket knife and inserted the blade into the lock, wiggling it back and forth, slowly twisting it against the tumblers. "I need a piece of metal, so I can make a key."

"Make a key? How can you make a key?"

"I saw a locksmith do it once."

"What kind of metal? How big?"

"Wait! That old cutlass we found in the main cave. That would work, I think. But I'll need a file."

Asa pulled his all purpose tool from the sheath on his belt. "There's a file in here," he said. "I'll get the cutlass."

Without Asa there, Ike felt more alone that he could ever remember. "We mean you no harm," he said, certain that the spirits were watching from above. "I give you my word that this place will stay the way it is. Asa's family owns this land and they can keep anyone out. Some scientists may come, but you can zap 'em if they get out of line."

"Who are you talking to?" Asa asked as he came back with the cutlass.

"The spirits. I want to make sure we're on good terms ."

He handed Ike the broken cutlass. "You need more light?"

"Yeah."

He fetched the lantern and watched as Ike stuck the flat steel into the huge keyhole and twisted it back and forth against the tumblers. Then he pulled the blade back out, and using the file, cut notches where the tumblers had left marks. Time after time he put the steel into the lock, pulled it out and filed away more metal. And then he stuck the makeshift key into the lock and turned and the lock snapped open.

They drew back the lid and for the first time in nearly

three hundred years the gold from the *Quedagh Merchant* and the other ships which Kidd had taken, lay exposed.

"How much is it worth?" Ike asked.

"I don't have any idea," Asa said. "I heard on the radio yesterday that gold is worth about three hundred and sixty dollars an ounce." He grabbed one of the bars and lifted it. Whoa, these things must weigh fifty pounds a piece."

"So that's fifty pounds times sixteen ounces, times three hundred and sixty dollars. My God, Asa. Each one of these bars is worth two hundred and eighty-eight thousand dollars!"

"It can't be ..."

"But it is."

"I think we're rich," Asa said. "There are five bars to a row, and I can't tell how many rows deep they go."

"That's what," Ike drew the numbers in the dust. "A million, four hundred and forty-four thousand dollars to a row?"

"You know," Asa said, "Maybe this is the time when we ought to tell our folks."

Ike grinned. "Sure have got a lot to tell 'em," he said.

They stood up and started toward the entrance.

"You think it's okay just to leave it here?" Ike asked.

"Been safe here for three hundred years. I guess it'll be okay for an hour or so longer."

"Wait," Ike said and he turned and walked back to the skeleton. Slowly he reached out and the instant he touched the skeleton's arm the moaning began, loud and threatening, but Ike did not let go, instead swinging the arm up onto the skeleton's chest, and laying it across the other arm. He let go and the moaning stopped.

Asa shook his head. "I was a lot braver when I thought it was just the wind," he said.

"But at least we know how to keep them from getting angry," Ike said as he joined Asa at the entrance. "You spend all your time reading about history. But I've been reading about the shamans of old and some of them had amazing powers. I'll tell you something else too. You know the skeleton we found with the hole in its head? That's where the moaning comes from. He was probably a shaman sacrificed by the shamans so his spirit would stay in the cave. The shamans were the voice of the spirits."

In truth, Asa did not know what to think. There was no question that the second Ike had touched the skeleton the moaning started and the second he had let it go, the moaning stopped. But this stuff about the shamans sounded just a little too wild. "Com'on," he said. "We've got a lot of explaining to do."

They worked their way out of the cave, trying unsuccessfully not to disturb the bats, and finally they climbed out into the sunlight and walked toward Asa's.

"Do you feel kind of strange?" Ike asked.

"Now that you mention it," Asa said.

"Kind of let down?" Ike asked.

"Something like that," Asa said.

"Weird." Ike shook his head and kicked at a loose stone, driving it into the brush. "We set out to find Kidd's treasure and now that we've we found it, I almost wish we hadn't."

"It's always that way when something ends. I felt the same way when we played our last baseball game this spring."

"And then finishing junior high. I never thought I'd miss

it, but I think I do."

"I'm gonna miss all the excitement of looking for the treasure," Asa said.

"Well, I won't miss Whitey or Fishbone, but the rest of the summer is gonna seem pretty dull." Suddenly he stopped. "Hey, wait! I got an idea."

Asa stopped. "Uh-oh," he said.

"No, it's nothing like what you think, Asa. We're gonna have to talk to reporters from the newspapers, right? And everybody is gonna want to hear our story. Suppose we don't tell them. Suppose we write a book about it!"

"A book? Us, write a book? Ike, I think you're three sandwiches shy of a picnic on this one. We're still just kids."

"Okay, so we get some help. I'll bet Miss Jameson would help, and we could even pay her to help. Or maybe some publishing company would help us. First we buy a computer and we write the book on that like we write stuff in school."

Ike, with an idea, was every bit as contagious as the measles, Asa thought. "What about the dirt bikes?"

Ike laughed. "You know what's funny? Now that I have all the money I'll ever need, I don't think I'll buy a dirt bike after all. What's even more amazing is that I can't think of what I'd buy. Except the computer."

Asa grinned. "Do you really think we could write a book?"

"Sure I do. I know we can."

"Well, you were right about Kidd's treasure, so I guess maybe you're right about this too, but for the life of me, Ike, I wish I knew what kind of a machine it is you've got inside your head that comes up with such wild ideas."

Ike grinned. "Imagination," he said.

About the Author

Robert Holland has a B.A. in history from the University of Connecticut and an M.A. in English from Trinity College. He studied writing under Rex Warner at UConn and under Stephen Minot at Trinity.

He has worked as a journalist, a professor, a stock broker, an editor, a writer. He hunts, he is a fly fisherman, a woodcarver, a cabinet maker, and he plays both classical and folk guitar.

While he was never a great athlete, he played with enthusiasm, and to some extent overcame his lack of natural ability by teaching himself how to play and then practicing.

Sometime during college, he decided to write, and has worked at it ever since, diverting the energy he once poured into sports to becoming not only a writer, but a writer who understands the importance of craft. Like all writers he reads constantly, not only because, as Ernest Hemingway once said, "you have to know who to beat," but because it is the only way to gather the information which every writer must have in his head, and because it is a way to learn how other writers have developed the narrative techniques which make stories readable, entertaining, and meaningful.

He lives in Woodstock, Connecticut with his wife, Leslie, his daughter Morgan, his son Gardiner, (when they're not away at school), and varying numbers of Labrador retrievers, cats, trout, and chickens.